B

BRINDLE

BOOKS

https://www.brindlebooks.co.uk

One For Sorrow

Sophia Moseley

Brindle Books Ltd

B

BRINDLE
BOOKS

Copyright © 2024 by Sophia Moseley

This edition published by

Brindle Books Ltd

Wakefield

United Kingdom

Copyright © Brindle Books Ltd 2024

"We must travel in the direction of our fear."
John Berryman, *A Point of Age*, 1942

The present day

The décor and layout of the bedroom was a combination of the necessary dull simplicity that ensured surfaces could be kept clean, with the more personalised comfort of a place that was meant to be a reassurance that the resident was a welcome and temporary guest, not a prisoner.

The flat plainness of clinical sterility was interrupted here and there with a tiny oasis of colour that had been added over time; a pretty picture frame here, or a little *objet d'art* there. She had been able to buy them herself in the clinic gift shop, and despite them being shatterproof, virtually unbreakable, thereby removing the risk of self-harm or harm to others, and being thick and sturdy compared to the delicate and intricately designed artisan pieces she was used to, they helped make the room her own.

The consultant had said it was important for her to understand this was not a place for her to stay for long, and it should be treated more as respite care, a temporary retreat. The clinic's success rate was the highest in the country; the longest anyone had stayed there had been twelve months – until now.

Charlotte had arrived at The Gables Clinic fourteen months earlier, and whilst the dissociative amnesia meant she couldn't remember much about it – how she'd got there, and what the first few days or weeks had been like, cut off from everything and everyone she knew – the Charlotte that had arrived back then, in the dead of night, was very different from the one she was now.

In the first few months, there had been days when she would have flashbacks; fleeting moments of recall, like she was watching a home movie that had been speeded up, so the images were momentary and brief. She found it frustrating, not being able to retain the memories long enough to make sense of them, a bit like a dream that you can only remember in snapshots. She would write down the memories she could recall, trying to pick out the important parts, justifying her impatience with the counsellor's assertion that each piece would join up, and when they did they would answer her questions, take away her doubts, and reassure her that her actions that had resulted in her incarceration were due to psychological manipulation.

With the help of her therapist and police records, it soon became apparent to her that those memories were false, and a manifestation of the stories she had been fed to increase her anxieties and obsessional fear; only then did she begin to let the images fade, accepting they did not represent the truth, and she slowly remapped her life.

She also learnt to compartmentalise and lock away events from her past that disturbed her. The coping mechanisms they taught her, along with the blend of drugs, meant she had been able to focus on the smallest of successes to start rebuilding her life; those fourteen months had seen a transformation from the unstable and irrational person she had become, leading to her being sectioned, back to the lucid, intelligent and insightful woman she had once been.

During the last six months, her medication had been slowly reduced, and when her behaviour remained steady, she was allowed more freedom to leave her room unaccompanied, and also, under close supervision, to go outside the building, albeit just into its gardens. The constant and strict framework of her daily life helped her to recalibrate and find a new starting point.

Between 2020 and 2021, there were 53,337 new detentions recorded in the UK under the Mental Health Act.

Today was Charlotte's last day in the clinic; she was sitting up in bed, the pillows plumped up behind her, looking around the room she had become used to and was now so familiar to her. They had said it was her own space, it would be her room for as long as she needed. But it had never truly felt like hers, there had always been a sense of it being a shared space; the whispers, dreams, and nightmares of those who had stayed before her lingered in the air. They say that the atoms we breathe in, which become part of us, were once part of someone or something else. That everything is borrowed, it's never *entirely* you or yours.

So, whilst the room was familiar to her, today it felt different, it no longer felt like *her* room. The sense of it being her refuge had gone. Tomorrow the room would be part of someone else's life, and whoever it was, they would breathe in the same air Charlotte was breathing out now, thus making her a part of whoever the next resident might be. This thought unsettled her; she imagined small parts of her being left behind. She wanted to take her all with her, leave nothing of herself behind in this place that had been both her saviour and her oppressor.

She gave a heavy sigh as her eyes roamed round the room, taking in the plain colour scheme on the walls, the position of the armchair in the corner, and her dressing gown, missing the cord, hanging on the back of the door. Whilst there was nothing different in the room, it had not changed since her first night there; the difference was in *her*. Today was a milestone day, and the start of her journey back to normal life. She just had to get through the next few hours, and then she would be allowed home.

She had got out of bed briefly in the early hours to go to the bathroom, obediently returning to her bed, and now waited patiently for the alarm to go off.

When they had set the alarm with her the previous evening, she had agreed she would not get out of bed, other than to visit the bathroom, until it sounded at 7 a.m., and despite having been awake since 5 a.m. she had happily stayed put, knowing that the consequences of doing otherwise would result in her release being delayed yet again. The pressure mat hidden under the carpet outside the bathroom door signalled to the desk how often and how long she was in there.

It had been six weeks since the last attempt to rehabilitate her; on that occasion she had become so agitated waiting for the alarm to sound that by the time it went off she was not only dressed and ready to go, but her anxieties had become so intense that she had lashed out at the nurse who went to pick up her bag. Had the nurse not been caught off guard, and had she not lost her balance and fallen on her left wrist, fracturing it, then it might not have resulted in the delay to Charlotte's release. But today was going to be different.

Most mornings, she would get up the moment the alarm sounded; she had never enjoyed simply lying in bed, even before her incarceration. She liked to be first in line for breakfast so she could choose what she wanted, and before the runny yellow centres of the eggs turned into solid plasticene discs under the hot lights. On the few occasions she had been late there was often just cereal or toast left; that was one of the incentives to get up with everyone else and be part of the community they tried to create. But this morning she allowed herself the luxury of listening to the gentle hum of the alarm, because today she was in control; today it was her decision alone whether or not she went to breakfast, and knowing she had that choice had a calming effect on her.

Her therapist had been right. Of all the people who had tried to help, including her mother and stepdad, the two people who thought they knew her more than anyone else, it was her therapist who had helped her through the darkest of days, and taught her how to control the unstoppable fear that was like a car crash going at full speed through her mind.

He had taught Charlotte how to control her fear; the crippling, utterly overpowering fear she had lived with for as long as she could remember. The kind of fear, if someone was minded to use it to control her, that stripped out any rational thought, and could be triggered by a single event, creating a spark in her amygdala, stimulating an excess of cortisol and adrenaline, making her heartbeat so rapid that it made her whole body throb, and fed her anxiety so that it overpowered the logical part of her brain.

Charlotte had suffered from hypervigilance almost her entire life, and despite therapy, medication, and various other less invasive interventions such as meditation, she hadn't been cured of the condition.

But with the help of her doctor, she had learnt how to deal with an episode, or at least keep its effects to a minimum. But it was after her marriage that things changed, and it was only when she looked back, she realised how her husband had manipulated her condition without her realising it. Whether it had been his intention all along, and he saw her vulnerability as an opportunity to achieve his aims, she would never know, and whilst she was learning to stop unearthing the past, a small part of her wanted to believe he had loved her at some point, loved her enough to not ignite her phobia, knowing that if it did happen she would go to a place that was deep within her subconscious. A state of mind that when aroused, would paralyse her in fear, at best leaving her disorientated; at worst, making her unable to discern right from wrong.

Then there was the place she went to after an episode; not physically, although she would often take herself away to somewhere quiet, to be alone; no, it was the place she went to in her mind, a dark, enclosed space that made her feel claustrophobic, its walls impenetrable and closing in, stretching as far down as they did up. But at the same time this would bring on a feeling of agoraphobia because the walls were infinite, an endless expanse of darkness, like space, where you could stare and stare, and never see the end of them, knowing they went on beyond forever, beyond anything you can imagine, into an endless darkness that was suffocating both by its closeness and also by its constant infinite shapelessness.

When this happened, she would fold within herself, into the abyss of her darkening mind, her body shrivelling to something indefinable, a powerless and weakened creature that shrank away from its surroundings, crouching in the corner, defenceless to the remorseless attack on her wellbeing. She would look up to see the light being slowly shut out as her fear became solid, a physical barrier, its geometric shapes sliding one over the other, until they completely cut out the light, leaving her alone in the endless perpetual darkness of her mind.

But now, with the help of the clinic's PTSD and trauma specialists, it no longer defined her. It would never leave her completely, but now it was just a very small part of her, small enough to be contained and controlled by the strategies she had learnt through the cognitive behavioural therapy sessions.

Now she was once more in control, making choices without fear of that blinding terror searing across her mind. The anxiety paralysis that had ruled her every breath was now controlled by her rather than her being controlled by it.

So, this morning, when the alarm had sounded, she'd left it to hum for its full minute, and when she heard the familiar three knocks on the door, she called out, 'Morning! I'm awake, but I won't be having breakfast this morning, thank you, maybe just a cup of tea later.'

The reply was slightly muffled by the closed door: 'No problem, see you in a bit.'

Charlotte recognised Stephanie's gentle sing-song voice. She would miss Steph; of all the staff who worked there, she had been the kindest, and whilst the staff were not supposed to become attached to any of the residents, Charlotte was pretty sure Steph saw her as the daughter she had lost in the first wave of Covid. When Steph's daughter had started university, it was her first experience of living away from home, and when the first lockdown happened, she had been persuaded by her boyfriend to stay in her student accommodation. But after seven days most of them, including her boyfriend, had gone home, and there was just one other person left with her in the shared house. Then, rather than admitting to her mother that she was overwhelmed by the isolation of lockdown, and asking her to come and get her, she had taken some of her flatmate's antidepressant clomipramine, and suffered a seizure. By the time they found her, it was too late ... because of Covid, Steph hadn't been allowed to sit with her daughter on the hospital ward, and could only watch through a window of the intensive care unit as the last few hours of her daughter's life slipped away. Since then, Steph had determined that no one would be left feeling isolated or alone, and she would only talk about a positive outlook on life, and how to find a way to beat the demons, no matter what.

By the time Charlotte had dressed and put into a bag the few belongings she wanted to keep, there was just half an hour before her taxi was due to take her home. She made her way down to the restaurant – now virtually empty – and sat at the table in her usual spot. The kitchen staff were busy clearing away the remains of breakfast ready to set up for lunch; she had watched them hundreds of times, and they all knew her and greeted her, but today she felt like a stranger. None of them knew she was being discharged that day, none of them would know just how different that made her feel. She stared out of the window watching the light and shadows as the sun intermittently dipped behind banks of cloud. Nothing had changed in the world; the sun still shone, the night-time came and went, people's lives had continued whilst hers had been put on hold. She was so deep in thought that she hadn't seen Steph arrive with two cups of tea. 'You'll be fine once you get back into the swing of things,' she said as she sat down opposite Charlotte and pushed the steaming hot tea towards her.

Snapped out of her daze, Charlotte looked up and smiled; as always, Steph knew just what she was thinking.

'I suppose so,' Charlotte said, 'but it's weird. From the outside, anyone looking at me would think I'm the same person, but on the inside I feel different. It's like Doctor Sullivan said – from the caterpillar to the chrysalis, and now the butterfly.'

Steph put her warm hand on Charlotte's and gave it a reassuring squeeze at the same moment the clinic admissions secretary came in to say the taxi had arrived.

At the time of going to press, the World Health Organization reported that worldwide there were more than 3 million people who died from Covid. Of those, at least 600,000 are likely to have died alone.

Charlotte aged fifteen

'Are we there yet? Are we there?' Charlotte asked, her eyes tight shut, and her voice nervous and tense. It had been several days since Laura had heard that level of anxiety in her daughter's voice. She had even started to hope things were improving and that Charlotte's obsessive fear was lessening, but as the exams got closer it became obvious that her terror was just as bad as it had always been.

If it had been just exam nerves, Laura wouldn't have been so concerned, and would have reassured her daughter that she just had to do her best; but her daughter's fear was less predictable and more crippling.

'Yes, love, we're here,' she said as she pulled up the handbrake. 'Now just focus; when you get out of the car, look at the school doors, nowhere else, just the doors. Don't take any notice of noises or shouts, keep walking until you're inside.'

'Okay, Mum. Thanks for being there for me.' Charlotte didn't look up as she pulled her school bag from the footwell, ready to get out of the car.

Laura smiled, putting her hand on her daughter's and squeezing it. 'You'll be fine. Just do your best,' she said, smiling at her daughter encouragingly, 'and when you've finished, check your work but don't look around, just keep your eyes down.'

Laura had pulled up next to the school gate, so Charlotte didn't have far to walk. Some of the kids from her class were hanging around outside with their boyfriends or girlfriends; a few of them teased her about her phobia, and as she made her way through the school gates a couple of them called out, 'Look out Charlotte, it's going to *get* you!' and then made hideous squawking noises. But she, used to it, ignored them. Compared with the fear she had been harbouring for as long as she could remember, the taunts were nothing.

As she neared the school entrance and the heavy glass doors slid slowly open, she walked quickly into the air-conditioned cool of the reception area, lowered her bag from her shoulder, and was at last able to look up. Her best and only real friend, Abbi, was waiting for her.

'You all right?' Abbi asked.

'I think so ... actually, no, I'm terrified,' Charlotte replied.

Abbi hooked her arm through Charlotte's and said, 'Come on, let's put our stuff away.'

Outside, Laura waited until her daughter had disappeared from view. She looked at the group of children who had called out to Charlotte and, not for the first time, resisted the urge to get out of the car and tell them what she thought of them, and say that they should be ashamed of themselves. But not after the last time, when she had reported the ringleader to the head of school. That had resulted in Charlotte being called into the head's office to accept an apology from the girl – who then made it her mission to pick on Charlotte even more. So, at her daughter's request, Laura had stopped reporting the bullying.

This was Charlotte's last term, and her final exams were just days away. St Willoughby's had been her sanctuary for so many years; from her first day in primary school, the staff had been patient and caring as Charlotte's phobia had grown with every passing year. They never judged or dismissed her obsession; they accepted it was more than just a fear, and that the sense of danger Charlotte felt could be so severe that it would stop her being able to carry out the simplest of tasks. They always offered support and help when needed, although since the new head, Steven Lewis, had joined a year earlier, he had changed Charlotte's pastoral care, insisting she should go outside every breaktime and making her sit in the main hall for exams, along with everyone else. He saw her fears as an exaggeration of a nervous reaction, which in his opinion she needed to overcome with self-discipline.

Laura had insisted he should speak to Charlotte's psychologist, who had said the additional stress of exam nerves was making her suffer from a condition called anticipatory anxiety. But the head assured Laura his theory was tried and tested in the battlefields of the Falkland Islands, and he was sure that Charlotte's nerves were no worse than those of a battle-fatigued soldier.

Whilst the psychologist did support the head's theory that continually avoiding what she feared most would make the situation worse, and gradual exposure would desensitise her, he wasn't convinced that the man, an ex-army captain, really understood how overwhelming and uncontrollable Charlotte's fear was. But with Charlotte's agreement, because she was so desperate to try and control her terror, they had agreed to give the head's plan a chance.

"The brave man is not he who does not feel afraid, but he who conquers that fear."

Nelson Mandela

As Laura drove away from the school she recalled, not for the first time, the weeks and months when she had determined to pinpoint the original cause of her daughter's phobia; there wasn't a day that went by when she didn't blame herself, and the relentless guilt-trips and beating herself up had soon taken its toll on her marriage.

Not that Iain had ever put much effort into understanding Laura's guilt; from the moment she had excitedly announced she was unexpectedly pregnant, it had been clear that he would never be a doting father. In fact, it was probably fair to say she had been a single mother from day one, especially when by six months old Charlotte was still not sleeping for more than a couple of consecutive hours at any time of the day or night.

When Charlotte was just a few weeks old, Iain had moved into the spare room, saying he needed to sleep because of the long car journey he had to make into work every morning.

Then his working days became longer, so he ended up seeing his baby daughter just at the weekends – and even then he made sure he was busy with *essential* DIY jobs, and the one time Laura asked him to look after Charlotte so she could meet up with friends, she passed him on her way into town as he was driving back from his mum's, with an empty car seat.

'Did you leave Charlotte with your mum today?' she had asked him later that evening.

'Yeah, you know how much she loves babies. They had a great time,' Iain replied.

'But I wanted you to spend some time with Charlotte, take some responsibility, maybe even enjoy being a father.'

Iain laughed. 'And I would have done – but that nappy? I nearly threw up just at the smell. There was no way I was going anywhere *near* that! It smelt so evil I told Mum to say a few hail Marys before she took it off.'

Laura turned and looked across the kitchen at her husband, incredulous that he could be so blatantly flippant and dismissive of the distress Charlotte would have felt sitting in a dirty nappy; and he knew, too, that his mum's deeply held religious beliefs did not always sit comfortably with Laura, which made his attempt at humour even more hurtful.

Iain was scrolling through the messages on his phone, completely unaware of, or perhaps deliberately ignoring, the icy quiet as Laura stopped doing the washing up, and turned to face her husband, water and soap suds dripping off her hands.

'What?' She glared at him, waiting for him to at least look up, but he carried on running his index finger over his phone screen. 'Are you telling me you drove Charlotte to your mum's without changing her? You made her sit in a dirty nappy that whole time? No wonder she had nappy rash this evening. Christ, Iain, just when are you going to start being a father?'

'A *father*?' Iain put his phone face down on the table and glared at Laura. 'How about when are you going to start being my wife again?'

Laura couldn't be bothered to reply, it was the same every time she questioned his behaviour towards Charlotte, which is why they now hardly spoke to one another, and their separate mealtimes were now a choice rather than a necessity.

Laura had tried to involve Iain, encouraging him to take on some of the jobs she did, expecting him to be equally excited by the joy of Charlotte's accomplishments. But they left Iain unmoved, and he would always say Laura did everything so much better than him, and how it would take her half the time it took him, and that Charlotte would sense he was nervous about getting things wrong – which Laura suspected he often did deliberately – and, Iain would say, it would upset Charlotte, which was *never a good thing before bedtime*. There was always an excuse, always a reason. Eventually Laura stopped asking for his help.

Now, every conversation ended the same way, until it got to the point where they didn't really talk, they just argued. The only time Iain showed any interest in Charlotte was when they were with family, and he would be the proud father taking the praise for anything she did.

Charlotte's development and progress was above average; by eighteen months she was already forming recognisable words and sentences, and each day her confidence grew.

But around the time of her second birthday her behaviour changed; she would suddenly become frightened without any obvious cause. It never lasted long, but it would happen apparently at random and without warning.

'The brain's ability to change in response to experience, is called 'brain plasticity'. In the first two years of life, the brain creates billions of new synapses, making 50% more connections than a typical adult brain. The connections that are not used are pruned away – a process called 'synaptic pruning'.
UK Trauma Council

It was a few days before Charlotte's second birthday, and Laura wanted to go shopping to get everything she needed for the party. Iain's mum, Sandra, had happily offered to look after Charlotte, and whilst Laura couldn't deny it was certainly quicker to get things done on her own, she didn't like to leave Charlotte with Sandra for too long, mainly because Sandra's religious fervour was verging on obsessive. Laura would take a small bag of books and toys with her on each visit but each time she picked her up, she would find the bag untouched on the chair where she had left it. And on the kitchen table, and on the low coffee table in the lounge, were large bibles, their pages dog-eared and worn from several years' intensive reading.

Laura knew that Sandra read her favourite verses to Charlotte, including from Leviticus and Isaiah, which talked about evil and punishment, and it always took several hours for Charlotte's mood to lift after a visit to her grandmother. Laura had tried to explain to Sandra that she was frightening her grand-daughter, but it made no difference; she would say it was important for Charlotte to have a balanced view on religion, and she was making up for the lack of religious education in schools – *and* home, she would say pointedly.

This time, when Laura got back to Sandra's house after her shopping trip, she noticed a small cut on Charlotte's hand, and asked what had happened.

'Oh, it's nothing,' Sandra said dismissively. 'We were out in the garden playing. I was only gone for a matter of seconds and when I came back, she was crying and rubbing her hand. I think she caught it on a bramble or something. I've cleaned it up.'

Having little empathy for an injury was one thing, but leaving Charlotte alone in the garden took Sandra's behaviour to a whole new level of neglect. This was because Sandra's garden was the least child-friendly place Laura had ever seen, with a pond, and a small shed with a broken door, piled high with gardening paraphernalia; and in the corner of the garden was a wild patch where she left nettles and thistles to grow in abundance.

Laura looked at the wound closely. 'It looks swollen. Are you sure it was just a bramble? How long did you leave her alone?'

'Oh, do stop fussing, Laura!' said Sandra. 'It's just a small scratch, nothing more, and it was a matter of seconds whilst I answered the door.'

'What? You left Charlotte alone in your garden whilst you went right through the house to the front door?' Laura's voice rose as her anger grew at her mother-in-law's irresponsibility. For someone who purported to be a devout Christian, she was the least caring or considerate person Laura knew.

'Yes, like I said, it was just a few seconds, a couple of minutes at most. Really Laura, don't get so worked up. Iain *said* you're letting things get on top of you – you need to relax more, or she'll be a clingy child.'

Laura was too angry to speak and knew if she did say something it would go straight back to Iain, so she put Charlotte in her car seat and left as quickly as she could. When she got back home, she took a closer look at the cut and was certain it wasn't just a scratch from a bramble; it was far too deep for that.

A few days later it was Charlotte's birthday, and both sets of grandparents visited for the occasion. Charlotte spent most of the afternoon playing in the sandpit Laura's parents had bought. Laura was just thinking of putting her to bed when she heard her scream.

She hadn't heard her scream like that before – she sounded utterly terrified – so Laura leapt to her feet, then ran over and knelt next to the sandpit. 'What's the matter? Charlotte, tell Mummy what hurts.' She scooped her daughter up and held her in her arms, trying to stop her sobbing, trying to work out what had happened. A bee sting perhaps? Or a sharp edge on the sandpit that had cut her hand?

Laura's parents, who had been standing nearby, reassured her that Charlotte had been perfectly happy, then had suddenly cried out for no obvious reason. Charlotte buried her tear-stained face in

Laura's chest and within a few minutes started to calm down.

Laura's mother knelt next to them.

'Did you see anything, Mum? What was she doing when it happened?' Laura asked as she stroked the back of Charlotte's head, trying to comfort her.

'There really was nothing, dear — she was playing quite happily. She just suddenly started to cry.'

By then Iain had arrived along with Sandra, who had come over to see what was wrong.

'She's just tired, Laura — why not put her to bed?' said Iain, as he crouched down and rubbed Charlotte's back in his attempt to comfort her.

'Iain's right,' said Sandra. 'It's been a long day, I'm completely shattered myself. Charlotte's just overtired, so get her off to bed. She's fine.'

Iain stood up next to his mum, both looking down at Laura who, whilst incensed by their impassive faces, had to admit she herself was feeling tired. But she knew all of Charlotte's cries, and this was a new one. She didn't want to make a scene, so she said her goodbyes to everyone and turned to take Charlotte inside, leaving Iain to bring the gathering to a close.

Laura was just about to step through the door into the kitchen when Sandra stopped them and reached out to Charlotte, cupping the side of her tear-stained face in her hand. 'Oh dear me, Charlotte, your mum *is* a worry-guts, isn't she? But she'll soon calm down when your brother or sister comes along.'

Charlotte tried to push her away, but as she did so Sandra took hold of her hand, and squeezed it where the cut was, making Charlotte whimper. At that moment, they heard the harsh raspy chatter of a magpie that was sitting in the cherry tree near the kitchen window.

It was out of Charlotte's line of sight, but Sandra turned her head to look at it then back at Charlotte, 'Now what do we say, Charlotte, when we see a magpie? That's right, we spit at the devil.' And she made a sound as if to spit.

Laura looked at Sandra, not quite believing she had said that, and wondered if she was trying to be funny, make a joke to try and get Charlotte to smile, but it was clear from the serious look on her face that she wasn't joking. 'Actually, Sandra,' said Laura, 'I'd rather you didn't say things like that. Charlotte's already upset, and you're not helping,' and she moved quickly inside before Sandra could reply.

Two days later, Laura was walking with Charlotte across the car park of the local village hall, where a playgroup for new mums had been set up.

Charlotte, a few steps ahead of Laura, suddenly came to a halt and started to scream and cry like she had on her birthday. Laura scooped her up and held her close, trying to calm her down, and only when the sobbing had subsided and they were inside the building did Charlotte loosen her grip. When Laura set her down on the floor, she kept her face buried in her mother's coat and held tightly onto her hand, only letting go when she saw her friends throwing bean bags into a bucket.

Shelly, one of the other mums who was standing nearby, came over. 'Problems?' she asked. Shelly and Laura had joined the group at the same time, and Charlotte had made friends with Shelly's daughter, Abbi, from day one.

Laura turned her head to look at her and smiled a hello. 'I'm not sure. That's the second time it's happened. It's just so weird. There's nothing wrong – she just suddenly screams out. It's like something has terrified her.'

Shelly looked across the room at Abbi and Charlotte who were busy sharing the bean bags between themselves before launching them back into the bucket.

'She seems all right now,' Shelly said. 'It could simply be teething, or maybe she's remembering a bad dream. Night terrors are quite common, apparently, at this age.'

The two women walked over to the other side of the room where a row of chairs had been put out for parents to sit and keep an eye on their children.

'Of course, they've reached the terrible twos.' Shelly continued reassuringly. 'At least you haven't had the tantrum in the shops yet. I'm dreading that.'

'Yes, maybe you're right,' Laura said, 'it's probably just a phase.'

But over the next few days, it happened three more times. Without any obvious reason Charlotte would suddenly cry out and get very upset. Laura's research only added to her worry; a sudden outburst could mean anything from hunger to a serious underlying medical problem. She recalled the conversation she'd had with her cousin about her son who was found to have a life-threatening heart condition that had been discovered only just before his third birthday, and she had ignored his complaints, assuming he was being a typical two-year-old. It was Laura's fear that Charlotte might have a serious medical condition that decided her to ask her doctor for help.

Fiona McCutcheon had been Laura's GP for her whole adult life. Laura had gone to university with Fiona's daughter, Rebecca, and the two of them had been inseparable. When Rebecca tragically committed suicide, Fiona shifted some of her maternal care to Laura, and was now far more than just her GP – she was her confidante and, of late, a shoulder to cry on.

Laura was sitting in the brightly lit room whilst Charlotte played happily with the abacus sticking out of a crate of toys.

'There's a lot going on in their heads at this age,' Fiona reassured Laura, having thoroughly examined Charlotte. 'I'm sure it's nothing to worry about. Keep a diary for the next couple of weeks, write everything down from the moment Charlotte wakes to the moment she falls asleep, and let's see if there's a pattern.'

Laura spent the next fortnight monitoring exactly when Charlotte became upset, noting down what she ate, drank, and played with, where they were, and what they were doing. When she went back to see Fiona, she had pages of notes.

'There's no pattern,' Laura said, 'it's happened six times now. She suddenly cries out and seems really scared with no obvious cause.'

Fiona looked at Charlotte, who was sitting on Laura's lap playing with a teddy, and whilst Fiona didn't doubt there was a problem, she felt sure there must be a simple explanation. 'We'll run a few tests; it could be something like a food allergy,' she said. 'Try not to worry, there *will* be an explanation. We'll find out what it is and get it sorted.'

Laura kissed the top of Charlotte's head and burst into tears. 'Sorry, I told myself not to do this today, but it's tearing me apart seeing her so scared and not being able to do anything about it. I mean that's what we *do*, isn't it? We make sure our children are safe, no matter what – that's our primary function.' Fiona pulled a couple of tissues from the box on her desk and passed them to Laura.

'I'm sorry, that was thoughtless,' Laura said. 'You know that more than most, but I can't *bear* seeing her so upset and not being able to help.'

Fiona smiled reassuringly, 'We'll get to the bottom of this – we'll get it sorted.'

But the allergy tests came back negative, so Fiona sent Charlotte for an MRI scan. This was the final hope of finding the answer, it was the most difficult and heartbreaking emotion Laura had experienced as she held her daughter whilst they anaesthetised her with a small amount of gas, then lay her motionless body on the bed for the scan.

Two days later Fiona rang Laura with the news that the results were back and there was nothing to see. Charlotte was completely healthy. There was no known clinical reason for her panic attacks. So Fiona eventually prescribed a mild sedative to try and suppress whatever it was that was causing the anxiety attacks, and within days things seemed to improve.

When the 28-day course had finished, Laura's nerves were primed ready. Just one week passed before it happened again.

The stress of it all was taking its toll on Laura, and she would frequently wake with a start in the middle of the night and sit bolt upright, gulping for air.

Meanwhile, Iain would often stay over at a friend's house for the odd evening. Eventually told her he was going to move out altogether.

'So that's it, then, is it? You're just going to leave us to get through this alone?' Laura leant against the bedroom door as she watched Iain packing his clothes into a large sports bag.

He stopped what he was doing and looked across the room at her. 'Didn't you ever wonder if *you* were part of the problem? Look at yourself, Laura! You've turned into a dull drab woman, you've let Charlotte wrap you round her little finger, you spend your every waking moment – and for that matter, your sleeping ones – thinking about her, until there's no room left for anyone else. You're cold towards me, you have been since she was born. I've tried, I've tried really hard to get close to you, I moved back into our bed, but I may as well have been sleeping with a corpse.'

His tone was mean and uncaring, but Laura was so exhausted, she no longer cared about the insults he threw at her. 'And that's what it boils down to, isn't it?' she said. 'You're not getting it. No matter I'm going through hell, no matter I've had no sleep since Charlotte was born, all you're interested in is having sex.'

'Okay, I won't deny it,' Iain retorted. 'I do miss it – but I miss you, the way you were, the way you looked, the things we used to do. They were and still are important to me, but you've changed completely, you're not the same person.'

'Of course I've bloody changed! What did you expect, that having a baby wouldn't change everything? That's the whole point! It's meant to change for everyone for the better – except, it seems, for you.'

Iain lifted the heavy bag off the bed and walked past Laura and downstairs. She heard him drop it on the floor and then heard him taking his jackets off the hooks in the hall. It was just after 10 a.m. Laura was still in her dressing gown, having just managed to get Charlotte off to sleep and was looking forward to a hot cup of coffee. She made her way downstairs, then halted on the bottom step so she was level with Iain, who turned to face her.

'You need help, Laura. Mum's offered to take Charlotte off our hands loads of times, but no one was ever as good as you when it came to looking after your daughter.'

'What's that supposed to mean, 'your daughter'? She's *our* daughter, Iain. And as for your mum looking after her, haven't you seen how she is with Charlotte? She terrifies her with her bible stories and tales of fire and eternal damnation.'

'They're just stories, Laura. It doesn't matter where they come from; the stories mum reads are no different from some of the ones you read. What about the granny-eating wolf, or poisonous apples? I'd say they were pretty scary!'

They stood in silence, Iain showing no sign of changing his mind or any regret at walking out on them.

'Get out, just go, Iain. You're a selfish bastard. I think you always were – I just never realised until now.'

Iain opened the front door and stepped out. Whether or not he was going to turn and say something more Laura would never know – she didn't give him the chance to say another word, as she closed the door after him and waited until she heard him drive away.

She headed back into the kitchen, made her coffee, and looked out across the small lawn, pulling her dressing gown tight around her. She watched the birds hopping about the lawn looking for food. A pair of magpies landed on the fence, their tails flicking and bobbing.

Two for joy, she thought ironically as they flew into a nearby tree, their black and white standing out against the soft green of the trees' new spring foliage, and as she watched their tails dip and flick, she had a sudden revelation. She rushed upstairs to grab her notebook, and checked the times of Charlotte's panicked cries:
Monday 2 p.m. sitting in rocker looking out to garden

Tuesday 10.30 a.m. in park on swing

Thursday 12.15 p.m. having lunch in kitchen, sat by window

Friday 3.30 p.m. sitting in garden on rug

Laura's heart was pounding as she flicked through more of her notes. There was the link! Every time Charlotte screamed out, they were either outside or looking outside. Whatever it was that was terrifying Charlotte was outdoors.

She quickly showered and dressed and waited for Charlotte to wake. Inevitably it turned out to be one of the rare occasions when Charlotte slept blissfully, unaware of Laura's excitement, and it was lunchtime before they went for a walk. They returned an hour later without incident, and whilst Laura was relieved her daughter hadn't been upset, she was frustrated at not being able to try out her theory.

But two days later, it happened. They were in the garden picking flowers when Charlotte gave a loud scream. Laura immediately picked her up and held her close to calm her and at the same time looked around for clues.

There was nothing obvious. The birds that had been hopping across the lawn earlier had flown away and the only sound was the cooing of woodpigeons, and the chatter of a magpie.

Laura walked around the garden with Charlotte in her arms, trying to find an explanation, but there was nothing. They spent the rest of the day inside, but Laura's determination to find the cause had renewed energy and she felt happier than she had done in a long time.

Iain returned a couple more times over the next few weeks to collect the rest of his clothes, and then brought a small van to take everything else that belonged to him. 'I'll leave the TV and spare bed,' he said. 'Maybe you could take in a lodger now the gym stuff has gone. There's enough room. Be good to get some extra money for yourself.'

Laura hadn't thought about money. With all her efforts going into trying to find out what was wrong with Charlotte, it hadn't even occurred to her how she would pay for everything without Iain there. Having given up a well-paid job in the city to become a full-time mum, she had come to rely on him paying the bills and the mortgage. The sudden realisation she was going to have to find a way of earning enough money just to live, let alone look after Charlotte, who seemed to be growing out of her clothes faster than ever, worried Laura, but the last thing she wanted to do was ask for Iain's help.

As if he knew what she was thinking, he said, 'Don't worry, I'll go on paying for things. But if you don't take in a lodger, you could get yourself a part-time job – probably do you good to get out of the house.' 'And away from Charlotte, you mean,' she retorted. 'Don't bother pretending to show concern for my well-being, Iain, it's all superficial. If you can continue to pay for things as you are, that would be ideal.' Laura's mood had shifted from feeling vulnerable and worried, to angry and resentful, and her resilience to cope on her own reignited her determination that she would not be bullied.

But her husband's reply was unexpected, and she felt the fire within her diminish: 'I still care for you, Laura, and despite what you think, I also care for Charlotte.' His voice was subdued, almost hushed. Laura could feel herself dropping her guard. Maybe she was wrong – perhaps Iain *did* have a point. She had been consumed with Charlotte's behaviour, even her friends had commented she needed to relax more. But she'd had no choice; Iain wasn't remotely interested in getting to the bottom of it.

'It's too late for that,' Laura replied. 'If you cared as much as you say you do, it wouldn't have got to this stage. You've wanted nothing to do with Charlotte since the day I told you I was pregnant.'

Iain shifted his position, pulled himself upright, the searching intensity of his eyes disappeared, and his tone altered. 'You're wrong, Laura. In the end, yes. I don't deny it, I couldn't continue. There didn't seem much point in staying with someone who'd become a stranger. All of this,' he gave a sweeping motion with his hand, 'creating the house of our dreams, it was for us, for you. I wanted to be with you for ever, and everything I did, I did for you, for us. We had plans, Laura, you and me, how it was going to be for us. But you cut me out, you removed me from your future and replaced my love for you with Charlotte.'

Laura's resolve stood firm. There had been too many times when she had backed down or simply kept quiet rather than have a confrontation. But not anymore. 'You moved into the spare room after just two weeks! I think you removed *yourself*, Iain, and the only time you showed any interest in Charlotte was when there were other people around.'

'I was getting no sleep, Laura,' Iain replied, trying to reason with her. 'I was virtually falling asleep at the wheel on the way to work. But you're right about when there were other people around. That's because it was the only time you didn't take control. It was the only opportunity I had to actually play a role in your parenting plan. You've done a fantastic job, you're a brilliant mother, and everyone can see how devoted you are to her – but you've let her take over your life. You exist only for her and no one else, not even yourself.'

'And there it is,' she replied. 'It's all about the way I look, for you, isn't it? Whether I'm attractive enough, turn you on. When we removed that element, there was nothing else left. Makes our marriage a bit shallow, don't you think? What about love, friendship, mutual support – all the other bits that make a relationship work?'

'I did try, Laura, I asked Mum to look after Charlotte so we could be alone, get back to being a couple again – but you wouldn't let it happen. The more you pushed me out, the more you made me feel like I was a spare part, superfluous to requirements. I won't deny I wasn't a natural father, but you wouldn't share anything with me. You didn't tell me what I had to do – you should have told me.'

'It's all my fault, then? I didn't explain the rules of being a parent, so you decide it's not worth the hassle of finding out for yourself, and figure it's easier just to leave?' Laura's voice was once again stronger, determined. She refused to take the blame for the collapse of their marriage, the break-up of their small family unit.

Iain sighed. 'Like I say, there was nowhere left for me to fit into your world. Maybe you'll find someone who understands how you tick, because I sure as hell don't.'

His tone was now cruel and cutting, but rather than make Laura recoil, it strengthened her resolve. 'Just *go*, Iain. We end up going round in circles, so there's no point in continuing this conversation. Shut the door on your way out.'

Laura turned and walked away; she couldn't be bothered with the fight anymore. There was nothing worth fighting for – their marriage had been over a long time ago.

As she headed into the kitchen, she heard the van driving away, but as she made a hot drink, she found herself thinking about what Iain had said. Maybe she *should* go back to work – perhaps it would help clear her mind, give her a different perspective, which could mean getting to the bottom of what was happening to Charlotte. Later that day she searched the job vacancies and started to research local nursery schools.

Within a few days, the idea of getting a part-time job had become a reality, and a nearby nursery was happy to take Charlotte three mornings a week.

'While typical fears disappear with age, the fear and anxiety elicited by maltreatment and other threatening circumstances do not.'
National Scientific Council on the Developing Child, Harvard University.

When Laura dropped Charlotte off for a taster morning at the nursery, fearing the worst and expecting tears and a refusal to let go of her hand, she was relieved to watch her daughter happily go with one of the teachers to meet the other children, and when she picked her up at lunchtime, any doubts she had were quickly removed. Charlotte had enjoyed herself and was looking forward to going back.

By the end of the second week, they had fallen into a new routine, with Charlotte going to nursery school three mornings a week and Laura working for a local solicitor. The number of panic attacks reduced, and Laura began to think everything was starting to work out.

And then, on the Friday of the fourth week, Mrs Elliot, the nursery manager, asked to see Laura: 'We think we've found out what it is that's scaring Charlotte.'

Mrs Elliot guided Laura to a chair on the other side of her desk. She was a young woman, articulate and attractive, her tone firm but gentle, and Laura imagined most children would do as she said.

Laura sat down feeling slightly on edge at the prospect of what she was going to hear. But her immediate concern was Charlotte's safety. 'What's happened? Is Charlotte all right?'

'She's absolutely fine,' replied Mrs Elliot with a warm disarming smile. 'She's a bright and very sociable girl, but with a phobia that completely overwhelms her when it happens.'

Laura felt a prickle of irritation – as if she didn't *know* how debilitating the attacks were! She wanted to ask Mrs Elliot if she had children of her own and if she understood how distressing it was to see your child in such a state and not be able to help. 'Yes, I *do* know that,' Laura replied, perhaps a bit too caustically, 'I've spent the last ten months trying to find out what's causing it.'

'Of course,' Mrs Elliot replied calmly. 'I wasn't suggesting you hadn't – but it's not always easy to find something when you're looking for it; sometimes it just needs a different approach.'

Laura's annoyance grew, and it was difficult not to feel stung by the young head teacher's tone. 'Okay; what have you found out?' she asked impatiently. 'We think she has a fear of magpies.'

Laura frowned and was stunned into silence; Mrs Elliot paused to give Laura a chance for it to sink in, then continued. 'There's a condition called ornithophobia, which is a fear of birds, but it seems Charlotte's fear is restricted to magpies.'

Laura said nothing but thought about all the times Charlotte had had a panic attack, and where they had been, and the more she thought about it, the more it made sense. 'That's interesting!' she said. 'But how can you be sure?'

'There's a pair nesting in the tree over the road, and they occasionally fly into the playground, usually landing on the fence, and we've noticed that each time Charlotte sees them, she gets very upset.'

'But why *magpies*?' Laura asked.

'I can't answer that, but something triggers a deep fear in her when she sees one. Perhaps speak to your GP; I'm sure they'll be able to help.'

But Laura wasn't listening any more. The pieces had suddenly slotted into place. She collected Charlotte and drove to Sandra's house.

As Laura pulled onto the driveway, she had already made up her mind she would never leave Charlotte alone with Sandra again, but meanwhile she wanted to know the truth.

Charlotte was asleep, so Laura left her and rang the doorbell. It wasn't long before Sandra appeared, and the exchange that took place was brief.

Laura asked her if the injury on Charlotte's hand had been caused by a magpie attacking her on the day she had been left with her. Sandra said nothing for a few seconds, just stared at Laura. Whether it was because she was unsure, or she was calculating what she was going to say, Laura couldn't decide.

Eventually, after a few moments' silence, Sandra shrugged her shoulders and said she couldn't be certain either way. She had given Charlotte a long bamboo cane to knock a magpie nest out of the tree, then the doorbell had rung, and when Sandra returned to the garden, Charlotte was running up the path crying and rubbing her hand.

Laura was numb with anger. 'No wonder Iain's like he is with a mother like you. Supposing it had been her face, her eye? Would you have shrugged your shoulders then?'

Sandra put her head on one side to look beyond Laura, and waved at Charlotte, who had woken up and was watching them through the car window, then said dismissively, 'You're over-reacting, Laura. Nothing like that *did* happen – and anyway it was ages ago, and it's all over now and forgotten.'

Laura snapped, 'But it's *not*, is it, you stupid woman! Charlotte could be mentally scarred for life because of what you did. I'll never forgive you for that.'

Laura couldn't bear to be near Sandra any longer. She turned away, too angry to speak, and hastened back to her car.

Having discovered the cause of Charlotte's phobia, whilst this knowledge could never remedy the situation, it at least meant that Laura had something tangible to deal with, and that meant she could look for solutions.

With the help of a child psychologist recommended by Fiona, Charlotte's anxieties became less intense. Laura also found a school whose pastoral care alongside their academic results scored highly, and when she found out Abbi was going there too, the decision was made.

Meanwhile, Iain announced he was moving to Edinburgh, to live with someone he'd met online, and within six months he announced they were expecting a baby. Laura wasn't sure which was the greater emotion: anger that he could move on so easily and father another child, thereby further removing himself from Charlotte; or pity for the woman who was probably expecting him to be a doting father.

Laura only allowed Sandra to see Charlotte at birthdays, Christmas, and other special occasions – and only when there were other people around.

At the firm where Laura worked, after several months and many polite rejections, she agreed to go out with Roger, one of the partners, and eighteen months later, they got married. It felt like things were finally working out.

The school proved to be the ideal place for Charlotte; the staff were caring and made special arrangements for her when she became overwhelmed, but they didn't cosset her. She flourished academically, and in her teens became captain of the netball and hockey teams. The head teacher had been there since the school had opened thirty years earlier, and her leadership and authority were the cornerstone of the school's success. No one could imagine it without her at the helm.

Which is why it was such a worry to Laura, when the head announced her retirement, that her replacement would be an ex-army colonel who would lead the school into the next decade.

By now Charlotte was fifteen and in her final year, and with the announcement of the new head, her anxieties started to resurface. Whilst she could still control them, it took all her effort and often left her exhausted, so Laura arranged to meet the new head in his first week of term.

He had charm and personality, and Laura imagined he would look extremely handsome in uniform, and when he took her hand in his, grasping it in a firm handshake, she noticed the ring on his third finger. On the cabinet behind him were photos of what she assumed were his young family, all of them very attractive and obviously athletic. *That's good*, she thought, *he's a family man, so he'll understand my concerns.*

Laura explained Charlotte's phobia, and how it had started, assuming he would not only have empathy, but would allow Charlotte's individual care to continue; and to begin with, Laura thought she had made him understand. But as he nodded and listened intently, asking questions, and drawing the full story from her, sometimes making her say more than she intended, she later realised he was covertly interrogating her.

When she left his office, she felt assured, but of what, she couldn't say.

He soon instigated a new regime of pastoral care and homed in on the strengths of the confident pupils, encouraging others to emulate them and match their behaviour, and he started to treat the playground more like a parade ground. Fortunately, he stopped short of saying that anxieties were a sign of weakness – but he failed to notice that his attitude gave the students who had previously been kept in check the opportunity to flex their muscles and bully not just the younger pupils, but also the ones they saw as an easy target. Including Charlotte.

During her final exams, her nerves were in tatters, and she found it difficult to concentrate. Abbi met her each day, either at the school gates or in the corridor that led to the main exam hall.

Recognising the disruption that some pupils were causing, the head put those individuals at the front of the hall, where the invigilator could keep an eye on them; after the exam, they were made to wait in the hall until the rest of the students had left. But even so, by the time the fourth and final week of exams had passed, Charlotte was exhausted and spent the next few days sleeping or listening to music in her bedroom.

As she moved through university, studying psychology and fine arts, the number of attacks became less frequent; by her twenty-first birthday, she was no longer seeing her psychologist, and Roger had turned out to be the father she had always needed; supportive, loving, and wise.

Sandra had moved to Edinburgh to be nearer her son, and whilst she stayed in touch, she rarely saw Charlotte. So it was a surprise for Laura to hear that not only had Sandra passed away after a short illness, but also she had left an exceptionally large amount of money to Charlotte.

'Paying her debt to salve her conscience,' said Laura when she read the letter Charlotte handed to her over breakfast. 'Probably all those deals she made with the devil.'

'Mum – that's so mean! But I never would have guessed she'd had that much tucked away. I'm not sure what I should do with it. What do you think, Dad?'

Roger, making another pot of coffee for them, turned his head to look at Charlotte with a smile. It still warmed his heart to hear her call him Dad. He hadn't ever asked her to – it hadn't entered his head she would consider him to be anything other than her mum's husband. But around her sixth birthday she'd asked him if she could, as if it was something very precious she had been considering for some time. His love for Charlotte was second only to the love he felt for Laura, and she had made his life complete.

'It *is* a lot of money,' he said, 'and putting aside what happened, she must have loved you in her own way. If I were you, I'd invest it until you've finished university.'

'Thanks, Dad, that's a good idea,' Charlotte said as she looked over to him and then gazed out of the window at the blossom tree. But her smile turned to a frown. Roger, following her gaze, saw two magpies. In those few seconds, the atmosphere in the room changed.

Laura, immediately sensing something was wrong, looked up, then turned her head to see what they were looking at. The news about Sandra had stirred up memories in her own mind, and probably in Charlotte's, and Laura was worried that the magpies might trigger a new episode of attacks. She turned to look at Charlotte, the adrenaline coursing through her veins.

'Two for joy,' said Charlotte, almost dismissively, returning her gaze to them both, only then realising what had been going through their minds. 'Don't worry, it's okay, I'm all right,' she said, smiling at them. 'Maybe it's a sign from Grandma – maybe she's saying sorry.' She reached across the table to put her hand on her mum's.

It was Charlotte's final year at university, and she was on target to get a First Class Honours. As she had followed Roger's investment advice, her money had increased in value by nearly half as much again. Everything was going to plan, and her future seemed settled. Which is why her surprise announcement in the spring caught Laura and Roger off guard.

When she rang them, they could tell by the tone of her voice something had happened, but she would say nothing more, only that she had some news to tell them, and she would be home at the weekend.

Laura and Roger went through every possibility: she'd been headhunted and offered a job abroad; she'd gone into business with someone and agreed to finance the deal; and the final thought – beyond anything they could hope – she was cured of her phobia, that her psychology studies had led her to find the answer they had been looking for.

When Laura and Roger opened the front door to welcome her, Charlotte's face was beaming. 'Hello, Mum and Dad,' she said, then turned her head and stretched out her hand, and from the side, beyond their line of vision, stepped a well-dressed young man.

Her announcement couldn't have been further from anything they'd imagined. 'Meet Toby,' she said. 'He's asked me to marry him, and I've said yes!'

Laura and Roger's face froze in stunned silence – Medusa herself could not have done a better job on them. Charlotte didn't notice their welcoming smile being replaced with a look of disquiet. But when you're in love, especially when it's your first love, you're enveloped by a warm, soft, comforting fug, which wraps itself around you, blinding you, tricking you into a way of thinking you have never known and cannot imagine ever living without.

Roger, standing behind Laura, tightened his grip on her shoulder just enough to reassure her; he too was thinking the announcement was unexpected. Perhaps that was why they felt the chill of a stranger and not the warm delight of meeting the man Charlotte wanted to spend the rest of her life with.

It took a few seconds for Laura and Roger to snap out of their stunned silence. Roger gave Charlotte and Toby his congratulations, and it was this subtle verbal nudge that propelled Laura forward to give Charlotte a tender hug. Then, with some reservation, she put her hand out to Toby, leaning forward slightly as they shook hands, so she could kiss him on the cheek. She stepped back, trying to appraise him without making it obvious, then said, with as much cheer as she could muster, 'Congratulations to you both – but don't let's stand here. Let's go through, and you can tell us all about it.'

As Charlottle led Toby past them into the lounge, Laura gave Roger a worried glance, but he smiled and said quietly, 'Come on, let's go through.'

They sat opposite Charlotte and Toby; Laura perched nervously on the edge of the sofa, her hands clasped together on her lap, with Roger next to her, discreetly watching Toby and listening intently to what Charlotte was saying. As a lawyer, Roger was well versed in holding his own counsel, and practised in observing and detecting the smallest detail, picking up every nuance and fidget that might indicate all was not as it should be. Both Charlotte and Toby seemed at ease, although Charlotte was clearly very excited, and wanted to tell them every detail of how they had met, whilst Toby kept quiet, waiting for his cue, as the events over the past few weeks were laid before Laura and Roger.

Laura sat stiffly; Roger knew, from her straight back and tense shoulders, that her face would be set hard and a small furrow would have formed between her brows, her eyes unblinking, as she listened to Charlotte. This was what it meant to love someone, to understand them without being told, and he couldn't help but feel that that element was missing between Toby and Charlotte. But he put his suspicions to one side for the time being, and gave Toby the benefit of the doubt.

Charlotte explained how Toby had joined the same chat group as her, and he was interested in the high end of art, and whilst he wasn't an enrolled student, he was more an academic enthusiast. Charlotte explained, with a gleaming smile: 'Toby prefers *autodidactic* – he thinks it sounds a bit more exciting.'

In the avalanche of words that came tumbling out of Charlotte, she explained Toby was hoping to work his way up in the company he was in, that he was their top salesman and he had a very successful investment side to the business. Toby interjected, 'And when I discovered the most beautiful woman on the campus was part of the same chat group, my life was complete,' making his feelings for Charlotte sound like second nature.

Charlotte leant back and kissed him tenderly. 'And that was three months ago,' she said, slipping her hand between his, which were on his lap, one hand clasped around the clenched fist of the other, his knuckles whitened slightly. He seemed a bit nervous to Roger, who had seen enough conmen in his career to know how easy it is to disguise true intent, and whilst Laura was concerned about Charlotte's happiness and mental well-being, asking Toby questions to learn what kind of person he was, Roger was analysing him for different reasons. He would be able to find out about his background easily enough, with a few online searches, and if need be, through his contacts in the police – but what concerned him was the part of Toby that was less obvious, what his motives were, and whether he was genuinely in love or if he saw Charlotte as an easy meal ticket.

Over the weekend, Charlotte tried to reassure them she knew what she was doing. She would continue with her degree; she wasn't foolish enough to throw away the last three years' hard work, even for Toby! She hadn't decided on her career path, but after they were married, she and Toby would carve a life together. He had no close family; he was an only child and his parents had died in a car accident when he was six, following which he had lived with his nan until he was seventeen, when she had died from a heart attack. So he was looking forward to being part of Charlotte's family, and having heard all about them and what had happened to cause Charlotte's phobia, he knew how important her family was to her.

By Sunday evening, Laura had warmed to Toby, and his reluctance to talk about the accident he'd had when boarding a train several years before, when his fingers got trapped in a faulty door, resulting in an injury that meant he couldn't feel the tips of his fingers, gave him a vulnerability that somehow reassured Laura of his sincerity.

She also learnt, with the work he did for a local estate agent, the money he earned would be enough to support them both until Charlotte found her dream job.

Later that night, Roger asked Charlotte if she had told Toby about her inheritance. Charlotte assured him that whilst Toby knew about it now, he'd told her he'd known nothing about it until after she'd agreed to marry him. He'd said he'd had no idea about her personal wealth, and was shocked when she told him. So, no, it wasn't her money he was after; they loved each other deeply, and it felt right. 'Remember when you first met Mum – you told me you knew within five minutes you'd marry her. Well, that's how Toby and I feel about each other. We just know.'

Roger smiled. She was right – he *had* known straight away that Laura was going to be the love of his life, and it was quite possible it was the same for Toby and Charlotte.

Over the next few weeks, Charlotte decided on her wedding dress and guest list. Through Toby's contacts, they found the perfect venue for the ceremony, an idyllic country mansion with a nearby chapel.

Whether it was her preoccupation with the wedding plans, or the years of therapy that were so well embedded, Charlotte's phobia was almost forgotten. Both Laura and Roger remarked how wonderful it was her anxieties seemed to be a thing of the past. She had told them that Toby was so worried about her having an attack, he had given her a silver pendant as a good luck charm, which he said had belonged to his nan – and she had led a wonderful life. So any time Charlotte saw a single magpie, she would touch the pendant to her lips and think only of their wedding day.

But Roger still harboured doubts: 'He just seems a bit too good to be true. So far, he hasn't put a step wrong. No one's that perfect.' It was just a month before the wedding, and he and Laura were looking at the guest list Charlotte had sent them. There were very few names on Toby's list, 'And this doesn't stack up,' said Roger. 'Someone as gregarious and socially active as him would surely have more friends than this. Okay he doesn't have any close family, but men like him generally have plenty of friends.'

Roger noticed a magpie land briefly on the fence outside the kitchen window before flying off again. 'And that pendant; I don't think it's silver, I'm pretty sure it's platinum, and that stone in the centre – I'd say it's a blue diamond.'
'Maybe he didn't want Charlotte to worry about wearing an expensive family heirloom,' said Laura, who had by now completely warmed to Toby.

'He knows how much Charlotte's worth, so I don't think he's worried about spoiling her with expensive gifts,' said Roger.'

'Who knows?' said Laura. 'Anyway, come on – let's go for a walk, stretch our legs before the weather changes.'

It was a week before the wedding. Everyone was too busy to notice how preoccupied Toby was, and they put his agitated mood down to wedding nerves.

When Toby had contacted the groundsman, Jason, the previous week to organise the job, emphasising it had to be kept secret, Jason had assured him that it wouldn't be difficult to catch a magpie and keep it caged until the wedding day. It was late June, and there were still some breeding pairs nesting in the estate woods, with the odd lone young male who had failed to find a mate.

To Jason, it seemed strange to go to so much trouble for a woman, but the money he was earning from this job would help satisfy his Bella, who had become increasingly demanding – even though he lavished her with gifts to keep her interested in him. His friends smirked with envy each time he walked into the pub with her, twenty years his junior, hanging off his arm like a playful kitten, and he was enjoying satisfying her constant physical needs – needs that his wife had forgotten years before he had left her.

'It's essential,' Toby had told him, 'absolutely *vital*, you release it at the right time.'

Jason decided to catch two of them, just in case one of them didn't survive being caged for the five days until the wedding.

He had set up a Larsen trap the previous day and was pleased to find a young male inside the cage, exhausted and wide-eyed with fright. Expecting it to struggle and peck at his hand as he lifted it out, Jason wore a thick leather glove, but the terrified bird was weak from trying to escape.

As Jason tied a piece of string to its stick-thin leg, he thought about Bella and whether she would be subdued if he tied her leg to something, but then decided it was far more fun having the excitement of the wild animal she became when they were alone. He didn't dismiss the idea, though, and tucked a length of baler twine into his jacket pocket.

He threw some more food pellets in the trap, and put the captured bird back in as well, tying the other end of the twine to the bar of the cage. Every time the magpie tried to escape, flapping its wings in a desperate attempt to free itself, it would rest for a few minutes before trying again, each time the twine pulling tighter on its fragile leg.

Jason watched it for several minutes, fascinated by its unceasing attempts to escape. He bent down and banged the cage with his .22LR Rimfire rifle. 'Stupid bird, you're going nowhere. No wonder they call dumb animals bird brains.'

He took a long drag on his cigarette, then blew the smoke into the cage so the magpie was momentarily engulfed in a cloud of toxic grey air. Jason coughed uncontrollably from the deep inhalation of the nicotine, swearing to himself as he spat a mouthful of phlegm into the cage. It landed on the magpie's back, the slimy bubble-filled mix sticking to its silky-smooth black feathers. He checked the trap once more, then moved off in search of rabbits to shoot. He thought he might skin a few, maybe enough to make a rabbit fur coat for Bella. *She'd like that*, he thought, *or maybe enough to make a rabbit fur rug for her to lie on ... I'd like that.*

The last few days leading up to the wedding were frenetic. Toby had organised the wedding cars; he was confident the high spec Ranger Raptor would go unnoticed amongst the catalogue of other vehicles that would be arriving on the day. The only difference was that he would be keeping the Raptor for himself; he would easily be able to convince Charlotte she had agreed to it, that they had talked it through, but in the excitement of the wedding she had forgotten about it. Toby had learnt how Charlotte's mind shut down when things got too much for her, and she had started to accept Toby's assurances that the things she forgot weren't important ones. He couldn't wait to try out the powerful twin-turbo 3.0 litre V6 engine.

There had been other investments he had persuaded Charlotte to put her money into – and so far, much to his relief, they had all given a good return. Toby knew Charlotte told her parents everything, and whilst they left her to make her own decisions, he guessed they would also not hesitate to protect her and her inheritance, no matter the cost, even if it meant doubting her future husband.

Roger's suspicions, whilst mostly satisfied by what he had seen, remained in the back of his mind. Although there was something about Toby's story that didn't make sense, he didn't want to detract from Charlotte's big day, nor worry Laura unnecessarily.

The night before the wedding, Charlotte and Toby decided to have a quiet family evening with Laura and Roger. Charlotte wanted to go to bed early, and for her wedding day to arrive quickly; all she wanted now was to be Mrs Stockton.

After a light supper and a few celebratory drinks, Toby headed off to the nearby pub where he had booked a room for the night, his last night as a single man. By the time he arrived, the first poker game was well under way, so he sat at the bar with a single malt until he could join the game.

Meanwhile Charlotte was going through her wardrobe once more to make sure she had everything she wanted for the honeymoon. Roger knocked on her door before opening it, and smiled at Charlotte's happiness, but he knew only too well how excitement could mask anxiety and doubt. 'You know, if you change your mind, it's okay,' he said to her.

'Whatever do you mean? What *are* you talking about? I love Toby! I want to spend the rest of my life with him. He makes me very happy, he understands my greatest fears and my longed-for dreams. But I'll never stop being your daughter.' She put her arms round Roger's broad chest, and he wrapped his arms round her, holding her close as he always had done to protect her.

'I know. I'm just saying, Charlotte, that no matter what, we're always here.'

He kissed the top of her head as she pulled away, saying goodnight to him and telling him he need not worry.

The house was finally quiet, and when he was sure both Laura and Charlotte were settled in bed, Roger went into his office and quietly closed the door behind him. Some information about the pendant had been discovered that needed looking into. He also needed to get hold of Toby's fingerprints without raising suspicion.

Charlotte lay in bed listening to the rain. It was a gentle fine rain – the kind you think you can walk through without getting too wet, only to find you're drenched within minutes. The forecast had shown clear skies, and they'd hoped so much for a dry day. She had been awake since dawn to watch the sunrise, wanting to absorb every second of the day, breathe in each moment so it became part of her very being. But as the different shades of pink and orange disappeared behind the grey of cloud, she felt her mood dip, until her phone rang.

'Good morning, Mrs soon-to-be Stockton.'

'Good morning, Mr Stockton.' She smiled at the sound of Toby's voice. It always made her doubts disappear, and, as if he knew exactly what was going through her mind, he said, 'Don't worry about the rain; it's going to pass in around half an hour, and then it's blue skies all the way to our honeymoon.' Charlotte smiled, and instantly felt better. She walked over to her wardrobe and gazed at the full-length Cartier dress hanging on the front of the doors, then ran her fingers across the lace and pearl bodice and down the silky-smooth skirt. 'I can't wait for you to see me in my beautiful dress,' she said.

'I can't wait to see you *out* of your beautiful dress,' Toby replied, his voice making her feel the most desirable woman in the world, 'I'm just going down for some breakfast, then I'll get ready to meet the woman of my dreams. Don't leave me standing at the altar, will you?'

'It's the bride's prerogative to be a little late, but I promise I won't make you wait too long.' Charlotte was about to ask about the car when she thought she heard something, 'Is there someone with you? I thought I heard a voice.'

'It's the family in the room next to me – right noisy lot, they've just gone down to breakfast, so I may wait a few minutes until they've gone. I'll see you at the church, looking utterly gorgeous. Bye.'

The green icon disappeared from Charlotte's screen. She stared at it for a few seconds, surprised by his abruptness, and was in two minds whether to phone him back. They were about to commit to spending the rest of their lives together, but the shortness of that conversation had left her feeling surplus to his requirements. She tapped on his name, but it went straight to his voicemail.

The landlord of the pub where Toby was staying knew that all the rooms were occupied, which meant the dining room was going to be busy this morning. He noticed to his surprise that the key to room 15 was still hanging on the rack, and checked the register. Toby Stockton's name was listed against it. The landlord knew Stockton was there – he'd seen him last night, waiting to join the card game. Stella had been left to lock up, so she'd know where Stockton had gone, not that it mattered to him; Stockton had paid his bill, and if he hadn't slept in his room last night, that was one less room to clean. But Stella would need a talking-to, because the empty glasses were still on the bar, unwashed, and the bar stool had been left lying on the floor.

Toby rolled onto his side in the kingsize bed, 'You really need to learn when to keep your mouth shut.'

'And you're just the man to do it,' Stella said, as she pulled him on top of her, and opened her legs so she could feel his growing hardness against her.

The previous night, after the card game, Toby had stayed in the bar long after everyone had left, and after he had told Stella he was getting married the next day to the most beautiful woman in the world, she had no hesitation in making it clear she wanted him, *now*. After collecting the empty glasses from the tables and putting them on the bar next to Toby, who was sitting on the bar stool, she turned to face him, leant forward, and kissed him, hard. Toby reached under her short skirt to discover she was wearing nothing underneath. He stood up and turned her to face the bar, pulling up her skirt and unzipping his trousers. The stool fell over with a crash that stopped them both.

Stella turned to face him – 'Best we don't make any noise, in here at least' – and led him out of the pub, across the car park and into her room, in an annex near the main building.

Toby hadn't known such an appetite for foreplay since he'd spent a night, some while ago, with a snake-tattooed tart and her friend. As he rolled onto Stella, he grabbed her wrists, pinning them to the bed, and with more force than she was expecting, pushed into her so suddenly she let out a cry. He released her left arm, and put his right hand over her mouth. 'What did I say about knowing when to keep quiet? You really *do* need to learn.'

Stella smiled underneath the restraining hand, promising with a submissive nod, that she would not make another sound. It was another fifteen minutes before Toby released her from his grip.

Charlotte sat on her bed staring out of the window; she had hoped Toby would sneak back into her room last night after everyone had gone to bed. She had stayed awake until well after midnight in the hope he would appear, but he hadn't. She had messaged him, *see you soon*, with a winking eye emoji, thinking he would understand the true meaning behind the message, but the message had remained unread until the morning, when he had phoned her. His phone must have been switched off overnight.

She put a pretty pink box on her bed and, removing the lid, carefully pulled the wafer-thin tissue paper to one side, uncovering a perfectly folded ash-pink Gilda & Pearl Harlow silk and gold lace babydoll negligée. She looped her fingers into the spaghetti-thin shoulder straps and lifted it out of the box. She was certain Toby would like it, and whilst dressing up for him made her feel cheap and tawdry, she had learnt what he liked, and she wanted to make him happy. It made a difference to how he behaved towards her. She would have worn it for him last night, but she smiled to herself at the thought of wearing it the coming night, their first night as a married couple.

The ceremony went completely to plan; the timings were perfect, Toby was beaming with pride when he saw Charlotte come through the chapel doors on Roger's arm; to anyone looking on, here were two people very much in love.

After the ceremony, the photographer took longer than Toby expected, and whilst Charlotte was too happy to notice the change in him, Roger could see Toby was getting impatient, and that he kept checking his phone. It was nearly four o'clock before they had finished, by which time even Roger had to admit he'd had enough. When they made their way onto the terrace to welcome the guests, nobody noticed Toby tapping a message into his phone – no one except Roger.

Jason looked at his phone and mumbled, 'About bloody time'.

He'd been told it would be around two-thirty that afternoon. It was after four. He had expected to be finished with this whole stupid job so he could go back to enjoy an afternoon with Bella.

He pulled the piece of sack off the cage; one of the birds was hardly moving. 'Well, at least there's still one left – that'll satisfy the crazy woman,' he said to himself as he grabbed the cage and walked out of the shed towards the edge of the woodland.

He set the cage down on a tree stump and opened the lid, grabbing one of the birds, and threw it up into the air, expecting it to fly away. But it landed on the ground just in front of him. He could hear the music coming from the wedding party, so quickly picked up the bird, checked it out, then tried again to launch it into flight. This time it flew away.

He spat as he turned back towards the shed, tipping the other bird out of the cage, and wondered why anyone would go to so much trouble for a woman. In his world, women were good for one thing only, and he was about to get something that was extremely good, for *him* at least. He picked up the cage, and sent a message to Bella, telling her he was on his way back, so she'd better be ready for him. He hadn't noticed that the other bird had recovered and was flying in the direction of the wedding party.

The guests had been making their way down the wedding line, shaking hands and congratulating the newly married couple. Roger had noticed the anxious look on Toby's face and how he kept looking at his watch.

The last of the guests arrived. Toby once more looked at his watch, then turned his head towards the woods that ran down the side of the estate, which is when he saw the single magpie, and said, 'at last' under his breath.

Charlotte turned to him and at the same time noticed the single bird. She gasped, and both Laura and Roger turned to see what was wrong.

The bird flew over them, its rasping chatter echoing across the garden. Charlotte looked at Toby, her face suddenly pale. Toby smiled, knowing she hadn't worn his good luck charm, because he had it in his pocket, and just as he was about to take it out to give to her, knowing it helped control her phobia, another magpie flew overhead. He frowned, but as he turned to look at Charlotte he put a smile on his face and said, 'There you are, two for joy,' and kissed her on the cheek. As they made their way inside, Toby tapped the screen on his phone, cancelling the final payment to Jason.

Charlotte smiled, the colour returning to her face. None of them noticed one of the magpies land on the ledge outside the second-floor bedroom, the room where Toby and Charlotte would be spending their first night.

Charlotte could not have been happier, whilst Laura's emotions were squabbling for space in her mind, from pride and happiness for her daughter, to fears for her safety and how Toby would be able to deal with any situation that might leave Charlotte vulnerable.

Roger's father-of-the-bride speech had people laughing, crying and applauding, and whilst he may not have been Charlotte's biological father, he was closer to her than Iain, who sat awkwardly a couple of spaces down from him. This had been the most difficult decision to make, and both Laura and Roger had hoped he would turn down the invitation – but at least his new wife wasn't there; at eight months pregnant with another baby, she had let them know she couldn't be there. And shortly after the wedding breakfast was over, Iain made a discreet exit. As the tables were being cleared, Roger surreptitiously removed the glass Toby had been drinking from, put it in a plastic bag, and took it up to his room.

Charlotte and Toby slipped off at midnight, and with their honeymoon flight in the afternoon the next day, no one expected to see them until late the next morning.

In the early morning Roger, despite his late night, wanted to clear his head before breakfast, so he went for a walk around the beautifully manicured gardens. He was just heading back, when he glanced up, to see Toby on the balcony of his room.

Toby kept his phone on silent and scrolled through the messages from Stella, deleting them all then blocking her. He looked at Charlotte, who lay blissfully unaware and asleep next to him. The silk negligee she'd been wearing was on the bedroom floor where he'd thrown it, one of the delicate spaghetti straps ripped off.

The doors onto the balcony were open, and the curtains moved gently in the breeze, giving glimpses of blue sky, which is when he saw the magpie crouched in the corner.

Without disturbing Charlotte, he slipped out of bed and went out onto the balcony. He tried to think how he could engineer this so she saw it, but when he picked the magpie up he realised it was injured.

When he heard Charlotte call to him, he decided he didn't have time to think about it, so without hesitation, wrung its neck and threw it into the bushes that ran along the side of the house.

He checked his phone once more before heading back into the bedroom, not seeing Roger walk across the lawn.

Roger raised his hand and was about to call out 'Morning', but instead stopped to watch Toby, who seemed preoccupied. Roger saw him lob something into the bushes that ran along the side of the house, before disappearing back into his room.

He couldn't make out what Toby had thrown, so he walked into the tall dark bushes to see if he could find whatever it was that Toby obviously didn't want Charlotte to see.

The only thing he could find was a dead bird, a magpie. He nudged it with his foot. It hadn't been dead for long – its head lolled uncontrollably – and one of its legs was misshapen, the claws shrivelled. If this was what Toby had thrown from the balcony, it was reassuring he was thinking about Charlotte. But something didn't feel right.

The final part of the celebration, when Charlotte threw her bouquet into the waiting throng, was met with a loud 'Hurrah!' Toby opened the passenger door of the Raptor, and helped her in, her beautifully tailored dress not leaving much room for manoeuvre, then they drove away, leaving the guests to bring everything to a conclusion.

Roger passed Laura his handkerchief so she could dab her eyes as they walked back into the house and up to their room to pack, ready to leave.

His phone was face down on the dressing table; he hadn't checked it since arriving on the Friday afternoon, and now he quickly scrolled through the messages. There were seven from his office – they could all wait until he was back at work on Monday – but one of them was more pressing; it was from the detective he had contacted several weeks before. But now was not the time to be thinking about what might have been discovered about his new son-in-law; right now he wanted to be there for Laura, who was both bursting with love and pride, and terrified for the well-being of their daughter.

They took the scenic route home, stopping off for lunch at an eighteenth-century coaching inn. Laura tried to stop checking her phone for messages, and whilst she was keen to get home, so she could be there for any emergencies, she also was not looking forward to going into the empty house, which Charlotte would now only visit occasionally. It was early evening before they got home, and found the handwritten envelope pushed through the letterbox.

Roger recognised Toby's handwriting and handed it to Laura, who tore it open, immediately going into panic mode. But the look of tension on her face soon faded, and she smiled as she read out loud the short paragraph:

By the time you read this, we should be enjoying the spectacular view across the Indian Ocean. Charlotte has told me so much about you both, I feel like I have known you all my life. I just wanted to reassure you, I will look after her with the same love and devotion you have done, and I am lucky to be part of such a loving family.

Laura passed the letter to Roger and said, 'I just have to stop worrying, don't I? It must have taken him ages to write this. It's surprising the train company didn't pay for an operation to fix his fingers, given it was their fault. But maybe there was nothing they could do. Anyway, you're right, I need to stop worrying.'

Roger smiled. 'You'll never stop worrying, it's your job. But perhaps worry a little less.'

The letter was a perfect touch – but perhaps a bit *too* perfect. In Roger's mind the chinks were starting to appear, and he had yet to be proven wrong when it came to a hunch about someone. But on this occasion, he hoped he *was* wrong. He tenderly kissed Laura on the top of her head, and as he straightened up and looked out of the kitchen window, he noticed the magpie sitting on the ridge of the fence, flicking its tail impatiently before flying off – which is when he recalled the dead magpie he had seen earlier that day.

There were too many coincidences; in his opinion, everything was being engineered. The good luck charm, Toby's agitated state at the wedding reception, the single magpie that flew over, then another; and the dead one Toby had thrown into the bushes. It felt like a scene was being set.

'The only item reported missing,' said the detective, 'was a piece of jewellery. She'd reported it following a break-in at her home whilst she was out with her grandson. When they returned, they saw that a window at the back of the house had been smashed. Her grandson checked the rest of the house, but it seemed they'd disturbed the thief before he'd had a chance to steal anything more than that one piece.

Forensics couldn't find anything to suggest the intruder had been anywhere else in the house. The report includes a note from her GP, who confirmed she had early onset dementia and was prone to forgetting things, and when the reporting officer asked where she'd kept the item, she couldn't remember – so it's quite possible it wasn't there in the first place. Other than that, the report says it's likely the burglar injured himself on the smashed window, as there was blood on a splinter of glass and on the paving stones outside it. That's as much as the police report revealed, and no one followed it up. Nancy Stockton died a short while after that, and her grandson, Toby Stockton, didn't pursue it. I'm afraid it joined the other 2.2 million unsolved crimes.'

'Thanks, Bill. I owe you a pint next time you're over here,' replied Roger. 'Just one other question. Were there any photos, images, fingerprints – anything at all – to identify Toby Stockton?'

'Only *her* fingerprints were taken, I'm afraid. They dusted down, to find one other set they presumed was Toby's, but as they couldn't trace him there was no final confirmation of that. They did a DNA check on the blood, but nothing came up. It would have been such a low-priority case, they wouldn't have gone to much trouble with this one. And after she died, and with no trace of Toby, everything was dealt with under the rules of intestacy. Not that there was much to inherit; she'd rented the house and had no savings. You'll probably find that her belongings were taken by the local house clearance. The only other incident that happened around the same time was an unidentified body found in the river not far from the property. It had been in the water several days and was badly decomposed. The coroner gave the cause of death as misadventure; and with no one logging a missing person, the body was given a code before the crematorium took it away. All I can tell you is he was male and aged around seventeen.'

'Okay, thanks again, Bill,' said Roger. 'Give my regards to Lucy and the boys, and let me know if you get anything back from forensics. Hopefully there should only be one set of fingerprints on the glass.' He put his phone down and logged onto his computer to look at his summary:

- Parents died 6 years old
- Raised by grandparent
- No other family, no photos
- Break-in
- One item stolen?
- Toby disappears
- Unidentified body found in river
- Nancy dies
- Five years later Toby resurfaces, working for Nelson Amalgamus

- What happened between the break-in / Toby's disappearance, and the time he started working for NA?
- What happened between NA and now?
- How many years before meeting Charlotte?

There were too many gaps, and Roger had noticed that Toby was adept at avoiding answering questions about his past. But perhaps it was simply that he found it too traumatic to remember and, just like Charlotte, had blocked parts out. But there was something in his self-assuredness that belied this theory.

An evening in November, ten years earlier

Adrian had walked quickly away from the house, knowing if he ran it would raise suspicion. He cursed his stupidity. Putting his hand through the smashed window had been a schoolboy error, because when he'd heard people coming in through the front he'd pulled it back too quickly, cutting his index and middle finger nearly through to the bone. He'd snatched a tea towel from a line to try and stop the bleeding, then walked towards the river, where he knew very few people went, and found a bench to sit on.

He hadn't eaten for two days, and as he sat down it started to drizzle. A magpie landed in the branches of a tree that were overhanging the river, its raspy chatter making him look up just as another one landed next to it. Adrian grimaced at the pain of his fingers, then picked up a stone and hurled it at the birds, saying out loud, 'Like *fuck*, two for joy.' He watched them fly away, and not for the first time wondered how, after being given a chance to do something with his life, he had reached rock bottom.

How had he changed from a bright articulate boy who'd won a scholarship to his grammar school to the homeless lowlife he was now? He had always blamed his foster dad, the constant pressure to achieve, always getting on at him about improving his marks – nothing he did was ever good enough. Until one day he'd had enough, and after being dropped off at school he waited until everyone had gone in, then started the long walk in the opposite direction to another life.

That was four years ago. He knew they'd looked for him and notified the police, but after twelve weeks the searching had stopped, and he was able to relax. He sometimes wondered, even though he tried not to, what his life would now be like if he hadn't run away from home.

His hand had stopped throbbing, but his head felt muggy. He leant forward, his elbows resting on his legs, his head bent. He didn't see Toby in the distance, coming towards him.

After checking the house and making sure his gran was all right, Toby decided to go back to the hostel. He'd called the police, and his gran told him he could go, she'd be fine.

He put the jacket she'd bought him for his birthday in a bag, along with his wallet and the birthday card, and while he wasn't sure about the pendant she had given him, he didn't want to hurt her feelings, so he'd dropped it into the bag as well. She'd told him it had always brought her luck, and now she didn't need any more luck, but he did – and she had pressed it into his hand. He smiled to himself and thought if he turned up at the warehouse with that hanging around his neck he'd never live it down; they already thought he was a bit different. If she asked, he'd tell her that, yes, he wore it; but she would most likely have forgotten about it by tomorrow, lately her memory loss had got far worse. He headed back along the embankment.

Then as he approached the weir he saw someone sitting hunched forward on a bench, head in hands. He walked slowly forwards, his senses primed. Not that Toby had ever been much of a fighter – he was all for avoiding confrontation – but adrenaline was coursing through his veins, because surely *this* was the intruder. He stopped just short of the bench, and stared at the man sitting there, who raised his head then stood up. Toby saw, wrapped around one hand, what looked like a tea towel. And it was soaked in blood.

His rage exploded and he lunged forwards, but the man was quicker than him, and the punch to the side of Toby's face, catching him unawares, knocked him back. As he stumbled to regain his balance, he felt his shins being kicked, the pain so intense he cried out as he fell to the ground, but then he was being pulled up again and he was face to face with the man whose breathing was heavy and smelt of sick.

Toby could barely stand, and fear had replaced his anger, he felt the wet of spit as the man said, 'What's your problem? I don't want to hurt you, just fuck off and leave me alone.' And he gave Toby a shove, not realising how close to the river they were, and Toby fell back into the water.

Then Adrian called out, 'Maybe *that*'ll help cool your temper down.' He stood for a minute, waiting for Toby to crawl out of the water, but he didn't. *Maybe he swam away*, he thought, as he picked up the bag Toby had dropped and took it back to the bench. Whatever was in there would be recompense for attacking him for no reason.

His hand was throbbing even more now. He looked around him to see if anyone was there to see what had happened, but the river bank was deserted.

He went through the bag and found a jacket, and a wallet containing a wodge of twenties. He whistled through his teeth, thinking, *Adrian, today's your lucky day after all.*

He found the birthday card and read the message:

Dear Toby,

Your mum and dad would be proud of you. Buy yourself a special treat with the money. Things will work out, you'll see. People forget after a while, and don't forget my lucky charm. It never failed for me. Good luck with your first driving lesson.

All my love, Gran x

Adrian tossed the card to one side and put the jacket on. It was a perfect fit, and as he stood up, something fell on the ground.

It didn't look like anything special, some kind of cheap bit of jewellery. He guessed it was the lucky charm, probably out of a Christmas cracker, but when he turned it over and read the inscriptions on the back, he felt something he couldn't ever recall feeling before – guilt. Because it was obviously valuable after all.

I will love you for however long I have left. 10 June 1944

I will love you for longer. 12 June 1944

He looked down the stretch of river where Toby had fallen, but there was no sign of him. Must have got out further along, deciding against another beating, and would be heading home. Adrian found a YMCA membership card in the wallet. He put everything into the jacket pockets and made his way into town.

As he walked into the YMCA hostel, he was relieved to see no one batted an eyelid. But as he made his way into the lift, he realised he didn't know what room number he was looking for.

He went back to the desk and told them he had lost his key and flashed the card at the receptionist, hoping that the man didn't know what Toby looked like. Luck was on his side, because just then an argument broke out between two men, and the receptionist, who obviously doubled up as security, quickly swiped a keycard and handed to him, before racing round the side of the counter and pulling the two apart. Adrian reached over the top of the desk and swung the screen round so he could see what room number had been tapped in. Room 14. If the real Toby turned up, Adrian would say he'd been given the wrong key.

After the best night's sleep he'd had in years, Adrian found a clean set of clothes in the cupboard, and put a couple of T-shirts and pair of jeans in the bag to take with him; he wasn't going to risk staying in Toby's room any longer. As he walked through the foyer, he noticed there was someone different behind the desk; a young blonde woman with a snake tattooed the length of her left arm.

She looked up and smiled. 'Hello,' she said, then looked at the bag he was carrying. 'If you're leaving, you need to sign out.' She pushed a keypad across the top of the desk to him. 'And if you have your keycard, that'd be good.'

Adrian looked at her and, noticing the snake's tail coiled around the top part of her arm, wondered what her pain threshold was like. He passed the keycard to her and when she scanned it she said, 'Toby Stockton; you've been here a while, not that I've seen you, I only started here yesterday, but it's a pity I won't be seeing you again.'

Adrian smirked; she wasn't even trying to be subtle. He liked that, and once again he wondered about her pain threshold.

'I almost forgot,' she said. 'There's a message for you, from the job centre. They said there's no more work available at the warehouse, but they've found something else for you, and to call this number to arrange an interview.'

'Thanks,' he said, 'I'll call them sometime.'

'Good luck. And here' – she turned the message over, and wrote on it – 'that's my number, if you're ever at a loose end.'

Adrian put the paper in his pocket and left.

It wasn't difficult to take on a new name and identity. He was used to it by now, and if words didn't work, he always had his fists. The cuts had healed, but the ends of his fingers were numb, which made writing difficult. With the money from the wallet, he got a room in a house share and then, with no other plans, decided to call the number the job centre had given him.

Two days later he was working nightshifts packing boxes. It was a boring job, but well paid and no one asked him any questions.

By the end of the first week he had got into a routine, and was even starting to enjoy it. He hadn't bothered contacting the girl with the snake tattoo, but then found out she was friends with a typist in the company he was working for. The three of them spent long evenings in his room until the landlord warned him that unless he kept the noise down he'd have to find somewhere else to live. So, he did, and moved in with the girl with the snake tattoo for a few weeks, before he'd had enough of her obsession with a local news story about an unidentified body being found in the river. He wondered if it was the man who had fallen into the river that night – but he'd still been alive when he left him, he was sure of that, so he had no reason to feel guilty. But because the girl wouldn't stop going on about it, he moved back into the house-share, promising the landlord he wouldn't make any noise.

Several months passed and Adrian had completely taken on Toby Stockton's identity, and he not only felt confident but comfortable and entirely at ease in his new life. Any guilt he'd felt about Toby falling into the river had long disappeared, and with his growing confidence and wealth, it was easy to reinvent himself and become Toby. How long it would last he didn't know or care. Tomorrow was a mug's game – he lived for today.

He changed jobs several times over the next few years and ended up working for an estate agent; with his good looks and charm, he soon had a long client list. Whilst his methods bordered on the illegal, his boss turned a blind eye and paid him a regular bonus, and with more money came greater confidence; after four years, he had his own portfolio that included sourcing priceless works of art for some of the wealthier clients.

Through the typist, who was studying massage therapy at the university, he started hanging out with some of the students. The group he was especially interested in was the fine art students. He couldn't care less about the artists; all he was interested in was the value of each piece.

He was also interested in one of the students, who stood out from the rest; Charlotte Abbott was attractive, had a great body and was intelligent. But that wasn't what was attracting him. There was something about her that seemed disconnected, she had a vulnerability that he could tell she tried to hide, and he wanted to find out what it was. With vulnerability came a weakness.

There were just six weeks left of term, but he had already made a connection with her and the foundations were laid, *as she will be before the week's out,* he thought to himself.

Which is why, after chatting to one of Charlotte's friends who let on about the size of Charlotte's nest egg, he had not only persuaded her to go out on a date and tell him everything about her phobia, but with just one week of term left, he then persuaded her to move in with him, and on their first night in his flat, asked Charlotte to marry him.

Seven for a Secret

Two days after they had returned from their honeymoon, Charlotte was still glowing with happiness, and when she visited Laura for the day, her behaviour left Laura in no doubt; Charlotte was completely in love with Toby.

'Do you know what he does every morning before I get up?' Her eyes were sparkling with fun. 'He'll look out of the window and check there are no magpies, and if there are he'll open the window and scare them away. We've turned it into a bit of a joke, so even if I do see one on its own, we pretend there's another one hiding somewhere. Not that I've seen a single one since we've been there. Which is odd, because there was a pair of them when we first moved in.'

Laura smiled at the effort Toby was going to, and wondered how long it would last.

'He wanted to be here,' Charlotte continued, 'but he got an urgent message from work he couldn't ignore. He was really upset, but said he'd be here at the weekend come what may.'

'That's okay – there's plenty of time for us to get to know one another properly,' said Laura. 'Hopefully it's an easy fix for him, and he won't be late back this evening.'

But he was late, and bad-tempered as he walked into the flat. 'I'm going to have to carry on working. You couldn't make me a bit of toast, could you? I've not eaten all day.'

He bent down to kiss the top of Charlotte's head as she was sitting on the sofa. They had bought the flat outright with Charlotte's money, and turned one of the bedrooms into an office for Toby. He disappeared in there now, and shut the door behind him. Charlotte left a plate on the side piled high with thickly buttered toast, and went to bed.

When she woke the next morning, his side of the bed hadn't been slept in, and the toast remained untouched in the kitchen. He wasn't in his office, either. She tried phoning him, but it went straight to answerphone.

Charlotte threw away the toast and poured the tea down the drain, and whilst she waited for the kettle to boil, opened the curtains, which is when she saw the single magpie sitting on the lamp-post opposite. She looked around to see where the other one might be hiding, thinking about the game she and Toby would play if they saw a lone bird. But there was nowhere for one to hide. Normally Toby was the first one to open the curtains, but he wasn't there, and he still wasn't answering his phone.

She stared at the magpie, willing its mate to appear, then pulled the curtains across so she couldn't see it.

By afternoon she was unable to focus on the simplest of tasks and was about to call her mother when Toby rang. 'Hello Charlotte, look I'm really sorry, but something's happened – nothing to worry about, just a problem at work. I might have to stay late again.'

His voice helped calm her nerves, 'I was worried when you didn't come to bed last night, and you were gone by the time I woke up. Then there was the magpie on the lamp-post, which made it all worse.' Charlotte's speech had started to race as her panic set in.

'Don't think about it – in fact, just close the curtains!'

There was laughter in his voice, and it made Charlotte smile, 'I did, but it's made it very dark in here and it's not even three o'clock.'

'The perfect time, then,' said Toby, 'to open that bottle of wine we bought, pour yourself a large glass and forget everything. I have to go – I'll call you later.'

Charlotte looked at her blank phone screen, once again feeling like she had been dismissed, but speaking to Toby had calmed her down, so she poured herself a large glass and sat on the sofa in the dark.

She must have nodded off, because she woke with a start when she heard the front door bang shut. She looked at her watch – it was just after 5 p.m. – as Toby walked in and unloaded his pockets onto the counter.

'Crisis averted!' he said, walking into their bedroom to get changed. 'Now where that's bottle of wine?' Charlotte took another glass from the cupboard when Toby's phone, on the counter, pinged. She desperately hoped it wouldn't be another urgent message asking him to go back to work. She glanced at it, but all she could see was the name Kirsty and a small 'x' next to the name.

Toby came into the kitchen, grabbing Charlotte by the waist and twirling her round in his arms.

'Your phone just pinged,' she said. 'Who's Kirsty?'

'Haven't a clue. Should I?' Toby asked casually.

'That's who the message was from,' Charlotte replied.

Toby frowned at her and loosened his grip from her waist as he picked up his phone. 'Please don't read my messages, there could be something confidential. I think it's better if you don't monitor my phone.'

'I'm not monitoring it! It pinged, so I glanced at it in case it was another urgent message, and saw the name Kirsty with an x – and there shouldn't be anything confidential between us, we shouldn't have any secrets,' Charlotte said. 'I certainly have none. You know everything there is to know about me.'

Toby put his phone back on the counter, face down.

'There are no secrets between us, of course not – but there might be highly sensitive information being sent to me, and I would be in deep shit if any of it got out.'

'Like I said, Toby, there should be no secrets between us – and who's Kirsty?'

'She's the company accountant, looks after the biggest clients, and we were in danger of losing one of our most lucrative deals. She's been working virtually twenty-four hours over the past few days, so she was just letting me know it was all sorted.'

Charlotte said, unhappily, 'Seems an odd way for an accountant to sign off, with a kiss.'

'It's meaningless, Charlotte,' Toby replied casually. 'She signs off with an x for everyone, not just me. It's her way. You really need to relax more – you get so easily stressed at the smallest thing, always turning something very minor into something bigger.'

His voice had a patronising tone, which Charlotte picked up on. 'I don't think someone signing off with a kiss is a minor event, and you seem overly bothered by me looking at your phone.

Toby reached out again, this time his voice calm and soothing, 'Charlotte, I can assure you, it's meaningless. You have my word, there's no one in my life other than you. But you have to stop looking for things that don't exist, it's like the other day when we were in the supermarket when that woman happened to choose the same bottle of wine as me. You thought she was about to take me there and then! I think she was as surprised as I was by your reaction.'

Charlotte couldn't think what he was talking about. She remembered being in the wine aisle and Toby chatting to the woman next to him, and looking at them, wondering if they knew one another, but she couldn't recall saying anything. 'I didn't do or say anything, I don't know what you're talking about.'

Toby ran his fingers through her hair. 'It's okay to block things out, Charlotte, don't worry. She was fine about it when I told her you were under a lot of stress. I've noticed that's what you do sometimes when things get too much for you.'

Charlotte frowned; she felt sure she would remember it, but perhaps Toby was right; there were times she would block things out of her mind. But she would do it rarely, only when things got really bad. But maybe he was right, and she was getting stressed with her final exams coming up.

Toby reached round her to get the bottle of wine. 'Come on, I'll have some wine too, and let's start the evening again.'

When she woke up, Charlotte could see the sunlight shining behind the closed curtains. The empty wine bottle and glasses were on the bedside table. There was no sign of Toby, and she was surprised to see her sleeping pills next to the bottle. She couldn't remember taking one the previous night – she only ever took one when she was going through a particularly rough patch, and she hadn't had one of those in months. But it would certainly explain why she had slept so heavily and not heard Toby leave.

She checked her phone. There were no messages from Toby, so she tried his number again, but it went straight to answer.

Something felt wrong, she felt unsettled. It was like she knew there was something wrong, she could sense it, but it was hidden by a mist.

She put the phone down on the bed next to her and stared up at the ceiling. How could they have been married for less than a fortnight and already have secrets from one another?

When Toby had told her there might be occasions when he'd stay over at a friend's house if he'd had to stay at work too late, because he didn't want to disturb her late at night, she had told him, more out of spite than anything, that she was thinking of going home to her parents for a few days. But she hadn't meant it, and she'd hoped he'd insist she'd stay in their new flat. But it had been quite the reverse – he'd even said her going home was a good idea. He hadn't taken the bait; it was almost like he was ignoring her like a parent would a petulant child.

She opened the bedroom curtains and looked out, the bright sunshine had gone, and been replaced with a dull and drizzly day. She pushed open the window and leant out to look at the road below made dark by the overnight rain, which is when she heard the rasping chatter of the magpie as it landed on the lamp-post opposite.

Charlotte's eyes froze on its shiny black coat, watching its long black tail flick up and down. She could feel her pulse start to race, and as hard as she tried to think there was another magpie hiding somewhere, that there were in fact two of them, she couldn't stop the panic rising within her, which is when she saw the car pull up.

It had stopped too close to the building for her to see it completely, so holding onto the window frame with her right hand, she leant out as far as she could. It was Toby – she could see him in the passenger seat. She could see him lean over to the driver then sit upright before getting out of the car, slinging a bag over his shoulder. He bent back down, said something, then waved as the driver leant over. Charlotte's grip loosened as she felt herself falling backwards, the walls started to spin and close in on her, then she collapsed.

She could hear his voice; it was the way he spoke to her to calm her down. It was a gentle but firmly reassuring tone that he had learnt helped to pull her back.

When Toby had walked into their bedroom to find her crouched on the floor, he slung his bag down and went to her, wrapping his arms around her, trying to pull her back from the abyss. He hadn't ever seen her this bad, but he had to do something about it – he couldn't allow anything to happen to Charlotte, not now.

He carefully lifted her and put her on the bed, talking to her constantly, hoping he would be able to reach her. He spoke about their honeymoon, how perfect it had been, reliving each memory as he stroked her hair, until he could feel the tension in her body begin to loosen.

An hour passed. He could hear his phone, but he let it ring. He knew who it would be; she would have to wait.

It was another hour before Charlotte recovered. Her head was spinning and she felt nauseous. As she sipped the hot sweet tea Toby had made for her, she explained what had happened; about the lone magpie, which she was sure was the same one as before – it was like it was taunting her – and then she had seen Toby getting out of a car she didn't recognise. Who was the glamorous woman in the car? Where had he been? As the words tumbled from her mouth in a confused jumble, Toby held his arm around her.

'You have to stop getting so anxious about everything,' he said. 'That's why you took a sleeping pill last night – you were so wired by the time we came to bed. That's why I didn't disturb you this morning. I got up early to go to the gym, and got a lift back. You have to stop being so suspicious all the time. You're the love of my life, you must know that.'

Charlotte put the cup next to the empty wine glasses, returning to Toby's strong comforting hold. This was where she felt safe, he would keep her safe from danger; he was right, she had to stop doubting him.

'You should ask them to change the shower gel at the gym. It smells like a woman's perfume,' she said.

Toby laughed, 'I'll tell them they need to get something that smells more masculine.' He slid her down the bed, 'Or maybe I can show you how masculine I am.'

Charlotte was vaguely aware of the sound of the front door closing, and rolled over onto her side, and smiled, reaching out to feel the remnants of warmth from Toby's body.

A week had passed since her attack, and with Toby's undivided attention and a visit to her therapist, she had recovered from it.

Her university work had fallen behind, but with just a few weeks to go before her final exams, she was determined to make up for lost time.

The kitchen was as they had left it the night before, and when she looked at the calendar and saw it was the fortnightly refuse collection day, she heaved the bag out of the pedal bin, and headed down to the communal bin area.

The wheelie bin lid was heavy and difficult to lift, and as it swung open a bag lying on the top fell over, some of its contents spilling out. As she went to pick it up, she saw a letter addressed to Toby, his name handwritten on the envelope.

Charlotte didn't recognise the writing, so she opened it and read what was inside.

I think I got the best deal, shame it couldn't have lasted a bit longer, maybe next time. You've got some making up to do. Like I said, it's not goodbye, it's au revoir.

K x

What happened next would later be described as intermittent explosive disorder; the rage that surged through Charlotte's body was so great, it overrode her every anxiety, and the tension she felt was one of revenge. The evidence she now saw was enough to send an urgent message to her hypothalamus, and the fight / flight response kicked in. This time, it was fight.

Charlotte took an image of the letter with her phone and sent it to Toby with a message *Stop lying*. She put the letter back in the envelope and put it in her pocket. Such was the anger she felt, she was blind and deaf to anything else, and she didn't hear the sound of the magpie that echoed across the car park. Nor did she see the decomposing body of the magpie that was in the bottom of the bag with the letter, the congealed blood on its head where the pellet had entered.

By the time Toby arrived, Charlotte had packed her bag and was ready to leave.

'What the hell's going on?' Toby asked, a mixture of annoyance and anguish in his voice. 'Where did you find that letter?'

'What does it matter?' Charlotte replied, 'it's there in black and white, and presumably that's who messaged you that night. The letter's from Kirsty.'

'Yes, okay, you're right, it *was* Kirsty,' Toby replied. 'But that letter's from a long time ago, long before I met you. I've told her there's not a hope of getting back together. Charlotte, I'm in love with you, no one else.'

They were interrupted by a knock on the door, and Laura walked in.

Toby ignored her, his eyes fixed on Charlotte. 'Look at the postmark, what's the date?' Charlotte pulled the crumpled envelope from her pocket, but the damp and dirt from being in the rubbish bin made it impossible to decipher the date.

Laura said nothing but took the envelope from Charlotte and looked at it.

'You have to believe me, Charlotte,' pleaded Toby. 'I'd do anything for you, no matter what, which is why I've said nothing about this.'

He pulled his shirt up to reveal his waist where there were the remnants of a cut across his side. Charlotte and Laura stared at it.

'You don't remember, do you?' said Toby. 'That night when you saw the message on my phone, you wanted to take a sleeping pill, but I said you shouldn't, and you lashed out at me with a knife. You don't remember, do you?'
Charlotte's eyes darted frantically between Toby and Laura.

'I think it's best if Charlotte comes home for a few days, don't you, Toby?' said Laura. 'Give you both some breathing space. I'm sure we can sort things out, but right now you both need to take some time out.'

Toby looked at Laura and nodded. 'Take what time you need, Charlotte. I'll be here waiting.'

He stepped forward to hug her, but she stepped back and followed Laura down to the car.

After two days of rest, Charlotte's confused mind had cleared, but she felt she still needed time away from Toby. So she decided to collect everything she needed for her final exams in order to study at home without being distracted.

By the time she and Laura left for the flat, it was late morning. It was unlikely Toby would be there, but even if he was, she would explain why she needed time away from him.

As they pulled into the car park, Charlotte looked around and was relieved to see his car was missing. 'I won't be long, Mum. You don't need to come in, I know exactly what I want and where it is, and I won't hang around.'

'All right, if you're sure you don't want me to help, I'll wait here for you. But call me if you need a hand.'

When Charlotte walked into the flat, it was like she was walking into a stranger's home – it didn't feel like hers. Something felt wrong, but she couldn't put her finger on it.

She went straight into the bedroom; everything she needed was in the cupboard, which is why she didn't notice the two near-empty wine glasses on the table in the kitchen.

The bed was unmade, but she was determined to simply get what she had come for and leave. When she pulled open the wardrobe door to see Toby's shirts hanging neatly, just as they were when she had left three days before, it was like everything had been frozen in time, nothing had changed. She knelt down and started to pull out the boxes of files and the books she needed, which is when she found the BB gun that had been tucked behind the boxes.

Charlotte sat back on her heels, holding the gun in her hands. Why was it there? Why would Toby need a gun?

She got up, putting it on the edge of the bed, and went over to her side and pulled open the drawer expecting to see her good luck pendant where she had left it. She wanted to take it back with her, but it wasn't there. She sat down on the bed and looked at Toby's side, imagining him lying there, reassuring her that everything was okay – and that was when she noticed the indentation on the pillow on her side, and the unmistakeable smell of perfume. The scent she had smelt on Toby before, which he'd said was the shower gel at the gym.

As her thoughts and fears raced to fill her head, blocking out all reason and logic, she picked up the gun. She didn't hear the door opening.

Laura looked at her watch. It was ten minutes since Charlotte had gone in.

Her phone rang. 'How's it going?' Roger asked.

'She's still there. She didn't want me to go in with her, but if she isn't down in a few minutes, I'm going up there.'

'Good. The sooner you can get her away, Laura, the better. I've found something out about Toby, and it's not good. Let me know when you're on your way home.'

'What do you mean, Roger? What's happened? I'm getting her now, we're coming home.'

Laura hadn't noticed that Toby's car had pulled in whilst she was speaking to Roger, nor did she know that Toby was heading up to the flat.

'Charlotte, what are you *doing*?'

The look in her eyes was not one he had seen before – it was like she was looking at him but couldn't see him. Her eyes were wide open, and her pupils so dilated, all he could see was the rich hazel brown of her irises. Her voice sounded distant, disconnected.

'She was *here*, wasn't she? Don't lie to me, Toby.'

'No one's been here, Charlotte, I don't know what you're talking about. You have to stop imagining things, making things up in your head.' Toby glanced around the room.

'What's the matter, Toby? Lost something? Because look what I found. I wonder what else you've been hiding from me?' Charlotte raised the gun.

'Charlotte, please put it down. I hid it because I didn't want you to see it. Each morning I would get up before you, I would wake up early enough to check outside. I was determined you would never see a single magpie. I kept that gun so if I did see one, I'd shoot it.'

'But there were always two magpies, you told me, there were always two, and one was hiding. Unless of course, you shot it, leaving just one for me to see. Is that it? Is that what you've done, Toby? I wonder what else you've done?'

'Nothing! You have to believe me, Charlotte.' Toby's voice was reassuringly gentle. 'Please put the gun down.'

Charlotte's head was pounding and her hands started to shake. 'I don't know what to believe any more. But I can't go on like this.'

Perhaps it was Laura's voice calling to her as she came through the door that startled her, because she hadn't meant to pull the trigger, and as the pellet hit Toby, he fell backwards, hitting his head on the corner of the cabinet.

The ambulance arrived within minutes and shortly afterwards the police, then Roger. With the information Roger gave them about Charlotte, she wasn't arrested, but was sectioned and at nearly midnight admitted to The Gables Clinic.

Two days later, Roger and Laura found that Toby had discharged himself from hospital and his phone number was dead. All his belongings had gone from the flat, so when Roger and Laura had taken Charlotte's things, they instructed the estate agent to change the lock and put it up for sale.

A few days later Toby's boss at Nelson Amalgamus asked Kirsty if she'd heard anything from him, and said that even if he did come back he'd be fired on the spot for faking the last two sales. Kirsty said she knew nothing, but as she touched the pendant that hung round her neck, she smiled to herself.

Also by Sophia Moseley and published by Brindle Books Ltd

My Time Again

Everyone turned to look at Kathy as she walked slowly past. She knew in her heart it was wrong. Her head screamed "No", but she went ahead anyway.

Have you ever wished you could undo a decision you've made? Return to that crossroad in your past and take a different path instead. What alternative life might have awaited you? And what of those you now know and love? Change what has been, and they might never exist at all.

Fate, which you cannot control, predetermines all events. Yet, your destiny is in your hands. Or is it? Which one is the dominant force?

Also by Sophia Moseley and published by Brindle Books Ltd

Unseen Follower

How many *friends* and *followers* do you have on social media? Tens, hundreds, maybe even thousands?

Hidden in the shadows of the digital realm, an ominous presence lurks.

In *Unseen Follower,* the virtual world become a labyrinth of secrets. A place where you cannot know who is watching your every click, tracking your every move.

The twenty-first century obsession to be part of the global social circle may lead you into the clutches of the follower who monitors your every post, every like, every share.

That person who glanced at you from across the road or stood behind you in the supermarket; you don't know them, but they may know where you live, where you work, and where you buy your coffee.

Do you know who's following you?

Based on real events, *Unseen Follower* will make you question who is.

B

BRINDLE
BOOKS

Brindle Books Ltd

We hope that you have enjoyed this book. To find out more about Brindle Books Ltd, including news of new releases, please visit our website:

http://www.brindlebooks.co.uk

Please feel free to contact us should you have any queries, and you can let us know if you would like email updates of news and new releases. We promise that we won't spam you with lots of sales emails, and we will never sell or give your contact details to any third party.

Our email address is:
contact@brindlebooks.co.uk

If you purchased this book online, please consider leaving an honest review on the site from which you purchased it. Your feedback is important to us, and may influence future releases from our company.

To view our current releases, please scan the QR code below:

Printed in Great Britain
by Amazon